I've travelled the world twice over,
Met the famous: saints and sinners,
Poets and artists, kings and queens,
Old stars and hopeful beginners,
I've been where no-one's been before,
Learned secrets from writers and cooks
All with one library ticket
To the wonderful world of books.

THE SMALL TEXAN

By tradition all Texans are giants among men, with the capacity for performing great deeds. Take the Rio Hondo gun wizard, Dusty Fog, as an example. At seventeen he commanded a company of Texas Light Cavalry. When the Civil War ended he became segundo of the biggest ranch in Texas, trail boss with few peers, town-taming lawman, and the fastest most accurate of the quick-draw breed. A Texan of the classic mould—except that Dusty stood a mere five feet six inches, but when the chips were down the small Texan stood the tallest of them all.

J. T. EDSON

THE SMALL TEXAN

Complete and Unabridged

ULVERSCROFT
Leicester

First Large Print Edition
published May 1983
by arrangement with
Transworld Publishers Ltd.
London

British Library CIP Data

Edson, J. T.
  The small Texan.—Large print ed.
  (Ulverscroft large print series: western)
  I. Title
  823'.914[F]   PR6065.08

  ISBN 0-7089-0956-6

Published by
F. A. Thorpe (Publishing) Ltd.
Anstey, Leicestershire

Printed and Bound in Great Britain by
T. J. Press (Padstow) Ltd., Padstow, Cornwall

For
Audie Murphy,
to whom Dusty Fog
owes so much

Part One

THE EVIDENCE OF HIS OWN EYES

GENERAL FRANK G. MANSFIELD had only been appointed as Governor of Kansas a month before, but from all appearances his term of office might come to a sudden and painful end.

When three of the hounds broke away from the line taken by the remainder of the pack, he followed them convinced that they were pursuing an almost full-grown cougar cub which had separated from its mother under the pressure of the chase. None of Mansfield's escort or companions saw his departure, as he discovered on looking behind, but that only added spice to the situation. If the hounds treed the cougar, he could claim it as his prize. Having hunted cougar on a number of occasions, he did not subscribe to the many highly-coloured legends of their ferocity and menace to human life. However, the three he was helping to hunt—a mother and two cubs—had developed too strong a taste for horse flesh to be left alive.

The trouble was that, instead of a one hundred and twenty pound Great Plains cougar, he found himself confronted by maybe six hundred pounds of very angry *Ursus Planiceps*. What set of circumstances brought a flat-headed grizzly bear from the Mineral country of Colorado into West Kansas, Mansfield could not imagine. It might have been a hard winter, following migrating game, or pushed that way in the course of a hunt. Whatever its reason for being there, the bear stood backed up against a blueberry bush and held off the hounds as Mansfield burst into view through the trees surrounding the clearing in which it decided to make its stand.

Steady though it might be under normal hunting conditions, the horse Mansfield sat showed a strenuous disinclination to facing that bristling, raging apparition. The unexpected sight also shocked Mansfield at a moment when he needed all his wits about him. With a roaring snarl, the bear charged at its new enemy and the hounds flung themselves aside to avoid its rush. Skidding to a halt, Mansfield's horse reared high on its hind legs. Before Mansfield realized what was happening, he slid backwards over

2

the cantle of his saddle, from the horse's rump and to the ground. How he missed catching the rear hooves in his face as the horse whirled around and fled, he never knew. What he fully understood, despite being winded by the fall, was that his mount was racing away carrying his powerful Sharps hunting rifle in its saddleboot.

No three dogs, even trained bluetick big game hounds, could hope to tackle and hold a full grown grizzly bear. However the trio sprang forward gallantly. One clamped its teeth on to the side of the bear's face, clinging there for a moment before a jerk of the great head flung it away. Attacking from the rear, the other two bit into the long hair on which they could obtain no grip. So the combined efforts of the hounds did nothing to slow down the bear's charge.

A man did not reach the rank of brigadier general at thirty-five, even in time of war, without the ability to think and act fast in the face of danger. Mansfield had attained his rank through courage, ability and presence of mind on a number of occasions. Confronted by as great a threat to his life as any from the late Confederate States' Army, he did not panic. With a desperate rolling thrust, he avoided the bear's attack, hearing its powerful jaws chop together behind his back and feeling one of its forefeet brush against his legs. Carried on by its momentum, the bear shot by him. Instantly he rose and raced across the clearing. If he could reach and climb a tree, he might be safe until his companions arrived or the bear decided to depart.

Behind him as he ran, the hideous grunting snarls of the bear mingled with the growling of the hounds. They still failed to halt the grizzly, for he could hear the approaching thud of its feet as it came after him. Darting a glance over his shoulder, he saw that he could not hope to reach a tree and climb high enough to save himself. While a Remington Model 1875 Army revolver rode butt forward in the cavalry-style holster on his belt, its twenty-eight grain powder charge lacked the power to propel a .45 bullet with sufficient force to save him.

Suddenly rifles started to crackle among the trees. The bear bellowed in pain and Mansfield saw it stagger under the impact of the bullets. Yet it neither fell nor wavered in its charge, being determined to repay the hurts it suffered on the closest living creature—and Mansfield qualified for that honour. Twisting around with his back to the trunk of a slippery elm tree, he watched the bear rushing nearer and could not spare so much as a glance at the men using the rifles. Yet he knew they were not members of his hunting party. At least three Winchester rifles and a carbine from the same company poured lead at the bear. Only one of his party carried a Winchester, the rest being armed with Springfield, Remington or Sharps single-shot sporting guns.

Not that Mansfield wasted time debating the matter. He could see the bullets striking, causing the long guard hairs of the bear's coat to jerk and wave as they arrived. Then he flung himself aside at exactly the right moment. Unable to stop itself, the bear crashed into the tree, teeth and claws sending chunks of bark flying in blind rage.

At which point Mansfield's luck seemed to run out. Catching a root as he moved aside, his foot slipped and he went sprawling. After clawing and biting its way erect up the tree's trunk, the bear loomed above him on its hind feet. Even as he grabbed at the Remington's butt, he saw a sight he would remember to his dying day.

A figure appeared, approaching from behind the bear; a man who definitely did not belong to the General's party. Six foot three at least in height, with a tremendous spread of shoulders that tapered down to a lean waist, curly golden blond hair and an almost classically handsome face, he might have been an old-time Grecian god. Except that no Grecian god ever wore a costly, wide brimmed, low crowned white Stetson hat, tight rolled scarlet silk bandana, expensive tan shirt, made-to-measure levis pants with turned-back cuffs hanging outside high-heeled, fancy stitched boots and a gunbelt with ivory handled Colt Cavalry Peacemakers hanging just right for a real fast draw in its contoured holsters.

Instead of attempting to draw his revolvers, the blond giant sprang forward. His hands went up under the bear's forelegs like a wrestler seeking a full nelson hold. At the same moment he spiked his boot heels into the earth and braced back with all his strength. Ample though the shirt's sleeves were made, they stretched almost to bursting point as his enormous biceps and shoulder muscles swelled and throbbed under the strain.

To Mansfield's amazement, the bear was halted in its tracks. Snarls of baffled fury rose from it and it shook its great frame to try to throw the man from its back. Mansfield realized that he must do something to help his rescuer for it seemed unlikely that even the blond giant's muscles could continue to hold the bear.

Then another man appeared, running towards the struggling man and bear. While a Texan like the big blond, the second rescuer seemed small and insignificant in comparison with the other. Not more than five foot six inches tall, the second man wore range clothes as costly as his companions' yet gave them the appearance of being somebody's cast-offs. Good looking, his face had strength and power if one chanced to notice it. Nor did the lack of inches imply a puny build. That small frame packed muscular development which would have equalled the other man's had they both been the same height. Around the newcomer's waist hung an exceptionally fine gunbelt, bone handled Colt Civilian Peacemakers pointing butt forward in its holsters. Small the dusty blond haired cowhand might be, but he acted fast and with decision.

With a surging heave, the big blond swung the bear away from Mansfield and towards the small cowhand. Skidding to a halt, the second man dropped his Winchester Model 1873 carbine. His hands crossed to the butts of the Colts and fetched the guns from leather in a single flickering blur of movement. Before the carbine landed at his feet, the small Texan's Colts roared. Held at waist level, aimed by instinctive alignment, they sent their bullets upwards to strike under the bear's snarling jaws and drive on into its brain. So close did the two shots come together that they could not be heard as separate sounds. Another rifle cracked in echo to the Colts' twin roar and its .44 bullet ripped into the bear's skull. The big body went limp, crumpling to the ground as the blond giant opened his arms and released his hold.

Slowly Mansfield turned his eyes from the quivering body and studied the men who gathered around it. He found his estimate of three rifles and a carbine to be correct. The owners of the other Winchesters proved to be Texas cowhands also and one of them was as eye-catching in his way as the blond giant.

Six foot tall, the man in question lacked the big blond's terrific physique. Yet, lean as a steer raised in the grease-wood country, he gave an impression of whang-leather toughness and controlled, latent, deadly speed. Under the black hat lay hair as black as a raven's wing and a face as dark as an Indian's yet young and almost babyishly innocent in features. His red hazel eyes did not go with the rest of the face. Those eyes had seen life—and death. He wore all black clothing, from Stetson, through bandana, shirt and levis pants down to his boots. Even his gunbelt followed the same sombre hue, supporting a sheathed ivory hilted James Black bowie knife at its left side and an old walnut handled Colt Dragoon butt forward in the twist hand draw holster on the right. In his hands he carried a magnificent Winchester rifle. As he walked, he gave one the feeling that he could cross a pile of eggs without breaking a shell.

Equalling the black dressed youngster in height and build, the fourth of Mansfield's rescuers had a pallid, tan-resisting face of studious, almost mild aspect. Like his companions, he wore the dress of a working cowboy and bore the indefinable air of a top hand. He had on an open jacket, its right side stitched back to leave access to the ivory handled Colt Civilian Peacemaker hanging in the carefully designed holster on his off thigh.

Black dressed boy, studious young man and blond giant were men to be noticed. Yet, strange as it might have appeared to an unknowing onlooker, General Mansfield directed most of his attention to the last member of the quartet. However, he saw more than a small, insignificant cowhand and the devastating speed shown by the other when drawing and shooting did not alone account for that.

Although they had served on opposite sides in the War Between The States, Mansfield agreed with the views of many Southern soldiers and regarded Captain Dustine Edward Marsden Fog as a man to be reckoned with. By all accounts which Mansfield respected, the small Texan called Dusty Fog had been a very able, chivalrous enemy. All unbiased reports from the Arkansas battle front confirmed that, even without Mansfield knowing that Dusty had volunteered to appear and testify at the court martial of the General's favourite nephew who stood falsely accused of cowardice and desertion in the face of the enemy. In addition to clearing Lieutenant Kirby Cogshill's name, the small Texan had killed a

10

much-hated Yankee general in a duel while behind the Union lines. As the general had been the aggressor, Mansfield did not hold that against Dusty Fog.

More than gratitude for the saving of Kirby Cogshill lay behind Mansfield's interest. With the War over, the small Texan had put aside his feelings about the Yankees and ridden on a very important mission into Mexico; the results of which had prevented what might have developed into open conflict between the two countries. Since then his name had gone far in the range country. Folks spoke of him as the segundo of the mighty OD Connected ranch, cowhand second to none, trail boss of the first water and town-taming lawman with few peers. Just how fast and well he could use his guns, Mansfield now knew. It was also claimed that he possessed strange bare-hand fighting skills which rendered bigger, stronger men help-less.

So, to Mansfield's reckoning, Dusty Fog could not be thought of in mere feet and inches. Mansfield had a special reason, apart from the saving of his life, for being pleased to see Dusty Fog. The fact that the small

Texan's all but inseparable companions were along increased the General's pleasure.

During the War, the blond giant Mark Counter had become known as a very brave fighter, while his style of uniform had been much copied—to the annoyance of many crusty senior officers—by the bloods of the Confederate States' Army. Currently his choice of clothing dictated what the well-dressed Texas cowhand wore. Yet there was more than an enormously strong dandy to Mark. A master hand with cattle, rich in his own right, he might have been the owner or segundo of a ranch. However he preferred to ride as Dusty Fog's right bower in the OD Connected's floating outfit. His strength and prowess in a roughhouse brawl attracted attention wherever seen. Less known was his true capacity with his matched brace of long-barrelled Colts. Men in a position to know claimed him to be a close second to Dusty Fog in both speed and accuracy.

Anybody who believed the black-dressed youngster called Loncey Dalton Ysabel was innocent or harmless need only mention the fact anywhere along the Rio Grande border between Texas and Mexico to be enlightened. Down on the bloody border folks knew *el*

Cabrito, the Ysabel Kid, to be just about as dangerous a *man* as that area ever produced.

Only child of a wild Irish-Kentuckian and a beautiful Comanche-French Creole girl, the Kid grew up among the *Pehnane*—Wasps, Quick Stingers, or Raiders to the white man—band of his mother's people. From his maternal grandfather, Long Walker, war chief of the Dog Soldier lodge, the Kid learned all the things a brave-heart warrior must know. Skill with weapons, ability to manage horses in almost any conditions, how to locate hidden enemies and follow barely discernible tracks, where to find food and water on the great Texas plains, all that and more he learned. The knowledge served him well as a member of Mosby's Raiders and later when he helped his father transport supplies run through the Yankee blockade across the Rio Grande into Texas. After the War ended, the Ysabels planned to continue their smuggling activities. Sam Ysabel's murder led to the Kid meeting Dusty Fog. From a youngster in a tough, illegal profession, with one foot on the slippery slope to out-and-out crime, the Kid became a useful member of Texas society. The training of his childhood served the community instead of being used against it. Not exceptionally fast with his Dragoon, he relied on the bowie knife at close quarters—being accounted a worthy successor to its designer in its use—and possessed an almost supernatural skill at handling his rifle over longer distances. The magnificent Winchester—which bore the proud, if modest, title "One of a Thousand"—came to him as first prize at the Cochise Country Fair and in competition with some of the best rifle shots in the West.

Although less known than his friends, Doc Leroy still bore a respected name among Texas cowhands. He had hoped to become a doctor like his father, but circumstances prevented him from completing medical school. Back in Texas, he took the only profession available in the years immediately following the War and worked as a cowhand with the Wedge trail crew. Very fast with a gun when required, he managed to avoid gaining a name in that respect. He still hoped one day to complete his education and learned all he could by helping doctors met during his travels. On the trail he set bones, removed bullets, attended to sundry illnesses and injuries and on occasion delivered babies. When the Wedge disbanded, Doc accepted

Dusty's offer and joined the OD Connected to ride with Ole Devil's floating outfit.

Hooves drummed and a fifth Texas cowhand rode up, leading his companions' horses and Mansfield's mount. Younger than the others, he was tall, well developed, with blond hair and a handsome face. He wore his range clothes as if born to them—which he had been—and the gunbelt about his waist carried its two staghorn butted Colt Artillery Peacemakers just right for rapid withdrawal. Young he might be, but his growing years had clearly been spent on the Texas range country and full of hard lessons well-learned.

In many ways the boy whose only name was Waco could be called a product of the times. Left an orphan almost from birth by an Indian raid, he had been raised along with the nine children of a North Texas rancher. Like any Texas youngster, he learned early to use a gun. At sixteen he rode as a member of Clay Allison's wild onion crew, with a brace of Army Colts in his holsters and a log-sized chip on his shoulder. Like the Kid, Waco might have become an outlaw but for meeting Dusty Fog.

On the day when the Rio Hondo gun wizard risked his life to save Waco from death

15

under the hooves of Allison's stampeding herd, the youngster's outlook began to change. He lost his truculence and watchful suspicion of others. Each member of the floating outfit contributed to his education, turning him from a trigger-fast-and-up-from-Texas kid to a likeable and useful young man. To Dusty he gave the loyalty and admiration that might have been his father's. In Waco's eyes, the small Texan could do no wrong. The guns Waco wore had been a present from his friends; a tribute to the fact that he now knew not only how to shoot, but when.

"I caught that hoss, Dusty," the youngster announced, dropping from the saddle of his big paint stallion. "Concluded to bring our'n along as well, knowing who'd get sent to fetch 'em anyways."

"You saved yourself another ride," Dusty replied and turned to look at Mansfield. He saw a tall, well made, good looking man with curly black hair greying at the temples and a neat moustache. "Howdy, General, we were looking for you."

"I'm real pleased you found me, Captain Fog," Mansfield replied. "In fact I intended to pass word for you to come and see me as soon as I returned to Kansas City. If you

16

gentlemen will be my guests for supper, I've things to talk over with you."

That night, seated around a table at the comfortable hunting camp, Dusty and the floating outfit learned the reason for Mansfield's urgent desire to meet them.

"I suppose you know why I was appointed Governor?" he asked.

"Way I heard it, to try and smooth things over between your folk and us Texans," Dusty replied. "And to try to do it afore all hell blows loose up here."

"Something like that," Mansfield admitted. "Kansas draws its income from farming and the railroad—"

"Leave us not forget the Texas trail herds," Dusty put in. "Farming won't support Kansas on its own and without our beef being shipped East, there wouldn't be enough trade for one train a week."

"I'm not gainsaying that," Mansfield told him. "However the behaviour of the trail crews is causing growing concern. So much so that there is an increasing pressure in the Legislature for strong measures to be taken to curb it. Up to and including prohibiting Texas trail herds from entering Kansas."

"You try that, General," said the Kid mildly, although the mildness did not reach his eyes, "and you're just liable to wind up without a State left to govern."

"I didn't say that I would agree to such a move, or even approve of it," Mansfield pointed out. "I merely stated that concern was expressed about the behaviour of the trail crews when they come to town."

"How's about the way some of those fighting pimps wearing the law badges in the towns behave against *us*?" Waco blazed.

"Boy's got a right smart point there," Doc went on. "Some of them'd make Mexican border *bandidos* look and act like church-going deacons."

"I've knowed some church-going deacons I wouldn't trust comes to that," commented the Kid.

"You bunch keep mum for a spell," Dusty ordered with a grin, preventing any further remarks on the habits and morals of church-going deacons or Kansas peace officers. He turned his attention back to Mansfield. "So some of the liberadical soft-shells* want you to get extra tough with us Texans, General?"

*Liberadical soft-shells: derogatory name for a liberal with radical tendencies.

18

"Let's just say there's pressure," Mansfield answered tactfully. "So I've been appointed and given the unenviable task of keeping the peace and satisfying everybody concerned." A wry smile twisted his lips. "It's not going to be easy."

"Easy!" Doc snorted. "I'd say it'd be near on impossible."

"There're times when I'd feel inclined to say I agree," Mansfield admitted. "My brother over in Arizona has it easy compared with what I've got on my hands."

"How come, General?" Mark inquired, having some idea of the problems which faced Mansfield's elder brother as Governor of Arizona.

"All he has to worry about is Apaches, Mexican *bandidos* and bad whites. I'm faced with the trail end town situation. Before I left Washington, that was raising almost as much heat in Congress as the anti-slavery issue used to."

"And among the same kind of folks likely," Dusty remarked, knowing what Mansfield meant.

First of the Confederate States to retain its solvency, due to its vast cattle industry, Texas already possessed men with the power to make their opinions felt at national level. So senators and congressmen from the Lone Star State raised their constituents' protests and thundered accusations against conditions in the Kansas trail end towns; hinting at wholesale swindling of the cowhands, while peace officers aided the citizens in open robbery or used violence and murder as a means of enforcing the law. In return, Radical Republicans and Liberals—full of bigoted hatred for all who failed to conform blindly to their beliefs—gave out stories of towns terrorized by drunken, rampaging mobs of Texas cowhands, or indiscriminate horse-riding and shooting on the streets endangering lives of harmless people.

One of the first tasks before General Mansfield was to discover the extent of the truth behind both sides' claims. That had been why he intended to send and ask for Dusty's advice. The small Texan knew the situation and the main cause of the Texan's complaints. Having handled the law enforcement in a trail end town, Dusty could also tell of the special problems which faced peace officers. Possibly he might be able to offer suggestions to help ease the tensions in an explosive state of affairs. Having stated his case, Mansfield asked a question.

"How much truth is there in the stories about cowhands' unruly behaviour, Captain Fog?"

"Some. But it's only rarely been as bad as the soft-shells make out. And even with the worst incidents there's been good cause behind them."

"Such as?"

"I'd say most of the incidents, hoorawing the town, shooing up the streets and such've been sparked off by some damned fool trying to cheat a cowhand."

"But they, the cowhands, do act wild in town," Mansfield insisted.

"Why sure," Dusty agreed. "Happen you'd understand why better if you'd ever been on a trail drive, General. Those cowhands've been working between ten and twenty-four hours a day all the way north. And that's not just riding up and down the line to make sure that none of the cattle stray. Time they reach the railroad and get paid off, they feel so relieved that they just have to rear back and howl."

"Most folks don't mind that, within reasonable bounds," Mansfield stated. "But it doesn't always stop at rearing back and howling."

"I know it," Dusty answered. "Thing that usually stirs up trouble is this. Those cowhands have money in their pockets, likely more than they've seen in their whole lives at one time. So they're set to spend that money and have them a good time. Only storekeepers, hotel owners, saloon bartenders, gambling men, gals, near on everybody wants to take it off 'em; and some aren't too choosy how they do the taking. So the cowhand raises a fuss about being cheated and the townie screeches for the law; which same's somebody like the Earps in Dodge, Jackley over to Trail End or Kurt Magus up to Triblet. They're fellers who rode for the North and still hold hates from the War. All of 'em're just waiting for an excuse to crack Texas heads from safe behind a badge. When the townie complains, the cowhand is pistol-whipped down or worse. That brings his pards in on the game. Us Texans tend to be a mite clannish, General—"

"So I've been told," Mansfield smiled.

"And they stand together," Dusty went on. "One gets hurt and the rest go out looking for evens. Then the hoorawing starts."

"You lay all the blame on the Kansans then?"

"Hell no, General. Handling a herd of over two thousand head of half wild longhorn's no chore for saints or soft-butted mammy's boys. Some of the trail hands are as mean as all hell and bad to boot; but most're just hard-working decent-reared young fellers out for fun—"

"Racing through the streets on horses, or shooting up a town?" Mansfield asked. "Breaking up a saloon, or roping folks as they walk by?"

"Most times a rope, gun and horse's the only things a cowhand owns to play with," Dusty pointed out. "But they always pay well for any damage they do and only ask to be treated halfway fair."

"I could tell you a few things about Kansas folks—" Mark began.

"And the folks who are putting the pressure on can tell me about Texans," Mansfield reminded him. "I want to get at the facts for myself so that I can assess the situation and decide what to do."

"You mean you'd like to see what goes on in a trail end town, General?" Dusty asked with the quiet tone which his friends knew meant an idea had come to him.

"I've visited Dodge and Trail End on the way out here for this hunting trip," Mansfield replied. "They appeared to be orderly, well-run places to me."

"You should see them as a Texas cowhand," Mark commented.

"How do you mean?"

"You went there as the Governor of Kansas," Mark explained. "The city fathers likely knew you'd be coming and had time to make sure that you saw only what they wanted you to see. Happen you went in unexpected, as an ordinary cowhand, you'd maybe see things a whole heap different."

"Which's what Dusty had in mind," Waco went on.

"Way I see it, General," Dusty said. "You're looking for a way to make peace between us Texans and the trail end town folk."

"That's true enough."

"And to do it, you want to see how much cause for complaint both sides have."

"I do. That's the only way I can answer allegations, or make suggestions for improving matters."

"Then why not come into one of the towns with me, dressed like a Texas trail hand and without its folk knowing who you are. That way you'll see things from our side and have an idea what goes on."

"All right," Mansfield answered and the Texans noted with approval that he wasted no time in deciding. "I'll do it. Which town do we go to?"

"They've seen you in Trail End and Dodge," Dusty replied. "I'm known in Mulrooney. That leaves Triblet, which's closest to us anyways."

"Triblet's bad, Dusty," Doc warned. "Maybe the worst of 'em. I've been there once with Wedge and know."

"If Triblet's the nearest town, we'll go there," Mansfield declared.

"It'll be riskier than all hell, General," Doc said soberly. "There's a real mean bunch running that town. Happen they learn who you are after you've seen what goes on, they'll not want you leaving to tell of it. You could disappear completely, or have to fight your way out."

"My escort'll be close on hand—"

"There's not enough cover to hide more'n

maybe one man at a place for a mile all around the town," Doc interrupted.

"Anyways, unless you can trust every last one of 'em, we'll not have your escort along," Dusty continued.

"Damn it!" Mansfield barked. "They're my men—"

"How long've you known 'em?" the Kid inquired.

"They're State Militia," Mark went on before Mansfield could reply. "Kansans born and raised, likely. Could be some of 'em'd reckon they should side with their own folk against us Texans."

Despite an inclination to stand by his men, Mansfield saw the point of the Texans' argument and admitted to himself how little he knew about the members of his escort. Maybe one or more of them might feel that loyalty to his fellow Kansans came before his duty; or could see a chance of making money by reporting the Governor's movements to the interested citizens of Triblet. In which case the visit would be a waste of time and might be used by his opposition in Kansas to accuse him of favouring the Texans.

"All right," he said. "We'll leave my escort behind. Tell them you're taking me after elk, or something. I'll be safe enough with you five along."

"There'll only be you and me going into town, General," Dusty corrected. "Doc's been there afore and might be recognized. Same with Mark and Lon, folks tend to remember them once seen."

"I could change my clothes—" the Kid offered.

"That'd be a real novelty," Waco scoffed. "They'd still recognize that mean Comanche face. Nope, there's only lil ole me could get by—"

"You'll be staying with the others," Dusty stated. "They'll be more likely to act up happen there's only two of us on hand. So you bunch'll hide up as close to town as you can and come a-running happen we need you."

"We'll be at least a mile off, Dusty," Doc warned. "Happen you want us all hid together. It'll be near enough five minutes afore we can get to you—after we hear the shooting start."

"That's a chance we have to take," Dusty answered. "How much can you remember about the lie of the land, Doc?"

Asking for a pencil and sheet of paper, which were found and presented to him, Doc produced a rough map of the town. After the slim cowhand finished his work, Dusty took and studied it. Picking out various salient points, he made tentative plans to cover their escape should the need arise.

Watching the faces of the young men around the table, Mansfield knew that they would follow Dusty's orders. He also saw why the small Texan could gain obedience from others with no thought of size. In Dusty Fog was that undefinable quality which made a leader, the kind intelligent men chose to follow no matter how tall or small he stood. Mansfield also realized that the rest of the floating outfit offered him a greater chance of security than an equal number of his escort. Every one of the Texans packed a life time of fighting savvy and skill with weapons. No man could ask for better backing in a tight, dangerous spot.

"I'll go along with you, Captain Fog," Mansfield declared when asked his opinion. "We'll play it your way."

"Thanks, General," Dusty replied. "We'll do our damnedest to bring you out of Triblet alive."

"We have to," the Kid went on. "Happen you get made wolf-bait, they might put some stinking soft-shell in as Governor. I wouldn't wish that, even on to a bunch of Yankees."

"It's pleasuring to know you've got my welfare at heart," Mansfield grinned, warming to the Texans. "One way or another, I'm going to learn something before this game is through."

Three days later General Mansfield stood among a scattering of large rocks something over a mile from the town of Triblet and changed into the clothing of a working cowhand. On approaching the town, the Kid went ahead as scout and returned with news that the nearest cover in which so many men and horses could hide was the place where they now stood.

At last Mansfield completed his changing and buckled on his gunbelt with the Remington in its holster. However the belt's polish had been scuffed and dirtied, while the clothes he wore showed signs of hard use. On Dusty's advice, Mansfield did not shave after separating from the hunting party. So his whisker-stubbled face added to his generally trail-dirty appearance.

"How do I look?" he asked the Texans.

Dusty and the rest of the floating outfit studied him critically.

"Moustache looks a mite too neat for a feller who's been on the trail," the Kid remarked. "And the hat don't set right."

"Best let me do it for you, General," Mark offered.

Reaching forward, the blond giant adjusted the Stetson—its brim and crown already shaped to the accepted Texas style—so that it rode at the correct jack-deuce angle over Mansfield's right eye.

"That's more like it," Doc said.

"Wouldn't say you'd fool a Texan," the Kid went on. "But you'll likely get by with those yahoos in town as long as you remember to talk right."

"Waal now, *amigo*," Mansfield replied in a fair impersonation of a Texas drawl. "I'll surely try to do that."

Grins came to his audience's faces. For three days he had been schooled in Texas terms and managed to sound like a son of the Lone Star State.

"I reckon you boys know what I want you to do?" Dusty remarked.

"Why sure," Mark agreed. "Wait here

30

unless we hear shooting, and if we hear it, get to you *pronto*."

"Wind's coming from town," Dusty continued. "You'll be able to hear it."

"Yes sir, Cap'n Fog, sir," the Kid agreed. "We'll be able to hear it for sure."

Dusty threw a glance pregnant with suspicion at the Kid. When that Indian-dark, baby-faced cuss sounded as innocent as a church pew full of choirboys, there was usually some mischief or devilment in the air. The fact that Mark, Waco and Doc also showed expressions of pure-hearted obedience did nothing to lessen Dusty's feelings of suspicion.

"Stay put outside town unless you hear shooting!" Dusty growled, studying each face in turn. "You hear me?"

"Why sure," Mark answered and the others chorused their agreement.

"Don't you-*all* go forgetting that you're not toting two guns," Waco warned.

"I'll try to remember," Dusty replied. "And don't you bunch go forgetting accidental-like what I said for you to do."

While Triblet lay farther west than the OD Connected found it convenient to bring their herds, Dusty took steps to avoid being recognized. He would be leaving his big, distinc-

31

tive paint stallion—with its OD Connected brand—behind and riding a dun gelding brought along for the purpose. Both the dun and a roan for Mansfield's use bore the brands of a West Texas ranch that specialized in raising horses and sold its stock throughout the State. They would not be connected with Ole Devil Hardin's great Rio Hondo spread.

Although Dusty retained his own clothes, he wore a gunbelt that carried only a single revolver in a cross draw holster. Close examination would show it to be a fine gun, of Best Citizen's finish and with the mechanism smoothed over to allow the extra split second of speed that sometimes spelled the difference between life or death. However Dusty hoped to avoid allowing the close examination necessary to show the Peacemaker's qualities. Unless he met somebody who was well acquainted with him, he felt sure that he could pass as an ordinary Texas trail hand.

Walking across to the dun, Dusty glanced at Mark's huge bloodbay, the Kid's magnificent white stallion, Doc's black and Waco's paint standing ready to be mounted if the need arose. Dusty hoped it would not. The dun and roan carried plain low-horned,

double-girthed Texas range saddles. To aid
the impression that Dusty and Mansfield had
come to Triblet ahead of a herd, they carried
no saddle guns. That and the lack of bedrolls
ought to give the desired effect.

"Let's go, General," Dusty said, swinging
astride the dun.

"Have fun," drawled the Kid.

"We'll surely try," Dusty promised and, as
he rode off with Mansfield, looked back at his
friends. "Now what in hell've that bunch got
up their tricky lil Texas sleeves do you
reckon?"

"How do you mean?"

"I know those four hellers. When they act
like butter'd stay hard in their mouths,
they're up to something."

"You think they might follow us into
town?"

"Not unless they hear shooting," Dusty
stated. "But they're sure planning on
something or other."

Failing to decide what that something
might be, Dusty put aside thoughts on his
friends' possible actions and looked ahead.
To outward appearances, Triblet seemed
little different from other railroad towns
which made the major proportion of their

living out of the Texas trail herds. Somewhat smaller than Dodge City, Newton, Trail End or Mulrooney, it offered the same general facilities for shipping cattle east, or spending the money earned driving the herds to Kansas. Shipping pens, all but empty at that moment, lined the railroad tracks on the side of town opposite to which Dusty and Mansfield approached. Where the pens ended, the town itself began. Along its curved main street lay most of the business premises; stores, saloons, other places of entertainment, the marshal's office, jail and various civic departments. Backing the street were the dwellings of the inhabitants, erected wherever the owners desired and without any thought of organized planning.

Sifter's livery barn, only place of its kind in town, was one of the businesses not based on the main street. It stood beyond the street's buildings, a large wooden structure with a big corral and water trough in front of it on the range side. Standing inside the open double doors, Eben Sifter watched the newcomers bring their horses to a halt and dismount. A sly grin creased his lean face as Dusty and Mansfield allowed their mounts to drink at the trough. In appearance Sifter might have been a professional gambler, for his fancy vest, frilly bosomed shirt and elegant trousers suggested the poker table rather than forking hay to visitors' horses.

Turning his head, Sifter spoke to the burly, hard-faced man leaning against the ladder which led up to the hay loft. After the other had taken up a Winchester and walked towards the front doors, Sifter left the building. Thumb hooked into his gunbelt close to the butt of the Colt hanging in a tied-down holster, he approached Dusty and Mansfield.

"You pair fixing to leave your hosses here?"

"Reckon so," Dusty replied.

"That'll be five dollars a day," Sifter announced.

"Sounds kind of high to me," Mansfield remarked. "Reckon we'll just take 'em into town with us, Sam."

"There's no leaving hosses tied to the hitching rails in Triblet, feller," Sifter warned. "Town ordinance says not. It stops the streets getting all fouled up with hoss droppings. Any hoss that's found hitched's taken down to the civic pound and held.

Then it costs you *ten* simoleons to get it back."

"What say we take the hosses out on the range and leave 'em Walt?" Dusty suggested, wishing to see how the owner reacted.

"It'd be cheaper," Mansfield agreed.

"Afore you go, there's the matter of paying for what you've had from me already," Sifter told them. "I'd say two-fifty'll cover that."

"Two dollars fifty just for letting the horses take a drink of water?" Mansfield growled.

"That's the price for it," Sifter answered.

"What if we tell you to stick your thumb up your butt and climb it?" Dusty inquired.

"I wouldn't like it," Sifter replied.

"Let's go, Walt," Dusty said.

"You try pulling out afore you're paid what you owe, and I'll have you tossed in the pokey," Sifter warned.

"You'll have us—!" Mansfield began hotly.

"Reckon you can make it stick, *hombre*?" Dusty put in, for his companion's voice showed signs of losing its accent.

"I'm a deputy marshal, duly appointed and sworn in, same as Elky there," Sifter answered, taking a badge from his vest pocket and nodding to where his helper leaned against the barn's doors cradling a rifle.

36

"Which same gives me the legal right to jail you happen you leave town owing money to a law-abiding businessman like me."

"Reckon we'd best pay up, Walt," Dusty said mildly. "Ain't no sense in getting tossed in the pokey afore the herd gets here."

"What herd's that?" Sifter asked, wanting to estimate the danger before deciding whether to go further in the matter of payment.

"A thousand head from the Running K and Bench O down to Rockabye County," Dusty replied, having come prepared with what he considered would be a tempting answer to such a question.

Not a large herd by Texas standards, handled by eight or at most ten men. Nor did either of the ranches named possess the reputation for salty toughness some others had gained. Watching Sifter, Dusty could see the calculation on the other's face. Then a sly expression crept over the man's features as he decided the marshal and deputies could handle that big a trail crew.

"Five dollars, you said," Mansfield remarked, hauling out a thick wad of money and starting to remove the top bill.

"Five a day," Sifter agreed, staring at

the money for a moment. Then he turned his eyes up to the sun. "Day starts and ends at noon. So if you'll be leaving 'em here after that it'll be another five."

"Damn it, this is—!" Mansfield spat out, but caught Dusty's elbow in the ribs as a warning to hold down his temper and retain the Texas drawl which was again beginning to slip. "All right, we'll pay."

"Yeah," Sifter grinned, taking the money held in his direction. "I just reckoned you might. Take 'em inside and put 'em away."

An avaricious glint flickered in Sifter's eyes as he watched the thick wad of money disappear into Mansfield's pocket. That was a fair sum of money and the small cuss might have almost as much on him. Yet Sifter knew that little more of it would come his way through the barn. Unless he missed his guess, neither of the Texans had been up the trail before. So they would offer easy pickings to various of the human vultures who made their living in Triblet. Long before the Texans returned to collect their horses, they would be plucked clean of their money.

There was, however, one way in which Sifter might obtain a further share of the cowhands' wealth and he decided to take it.

Waiting until they led their horses into the barn, Sifter turned his attention from the Texans to his employee. Telling Elky to watch out for things, Sifter walked off towards the town's main street.

Watching Dusty and Mansfield tend to their horses, Elky felt a twinge of disappointment. Experience told him what his boss planned to do and he knew that only the crumbs of the affair would come his way. Neither visitor's saddle held war bags or anything else that might produce loot. Elky scowled, feeling cheated, but said and did nothing.

Working faster than Mansfield, Dusty finished settling in his horse first. So he strolled from the building's big doors and looked around. To all appearances he might have been doing no more than contemplate the scene of hoped-for revels, but a grimmer purpose lay behind his scrutiny. If trouble came in the town, he hoped to reach the livery barn and use it as a base from which to stand off their attackers. With the wind blowing from the town towards his friends, they could hear the sound of shots easily enough. However it would, as Doc warned, be several minutes before they arrived and

Dusty wanted to make sure of being able to find a place where he could hold off an attack until they came.

From where Dusty stood alongside the water-trough, he looked by the end of the barn, between two other buildings and at the end of the Lone Wolf Saloon across the street which at that point made a sharp curve. Although surrounded on two sides by the homes of various citizens, none of them stood closer than fifty yards from the barn. Beyond the corral, five houses formed a rough line out on to the range. The farthest from town had a high plank fence surrounding its grounds, as if the owner wished to hide his activities from prying eyes. A number of horses moved around in the corral, partially shielding the barn from the buildings behind it. Off to the right, clear of other houses, stood a big old cottonwood. However the tree did not command a view of the water-trough. If they could not reach the barn's interior, Dusty concluded that they could take cover behind the trough. While not a perfect defensive position, he felt that it might serve their needs.

Seeing the anger on Mansfield's face as he left the barn, Dusty wasted no time in leading him out of earshot of the man inside.

"That was handled neat," Dusty commented as he and Mansfield approached the street.

"It was damned robbery!" Mansfield growled back.

"Why sure," agreed Dusty. "But you've got to admit it's done neat. On the face of it, that civic ordinance's reasonable. You've seen the way streets get fouled by horses being left hitched along 'em. Suppose you heard that a cowhand ruckus started because they didn't want to follow that rule and hadn't seen the barn owner's game, what'd you think?"

"That they were acting unreasonable."

"Or plain ornery. Only a cowhand, or anybody who comes here, has to use the barn, else chance seeing his horse hauled off to the civic pound. So that weasel-faced jasper charges as high as he wants and backs it with a deputy's badge."

"I'll say he charges!" Mansfield spat out. "Five dollars a day, no matter what time you arrive. It's near on half past eleven and we still had to pay for a full day."

"Yep!" Dusty replied. "And I'll bet you see more things like that afore we've done here."

Reaching the street, they paused and looked around. At that early hour everything seemed quiet, with little traffic and few people in view. Dusty led the way along the street and they paused to look into various windows.

"The prices are much the same as in Kansas City," Mansfield remarked.

"Maybe they change when you come to buy something," Dusty answered. "Only if we want to pass for trail hands just arrived in town, we'd best go across to that saloon and have a drink."

Crossing the street, they returned to the Lone Wolf saloon, a big, fancy-looking two floor building calculated to draw trail hands like flies to a honeypot. None of the games were open as Dusty and Mansfield entered and only one big, surly-faced bartender stood behind the long counter.

"Whiskey," Mansfield ordered, studying the line of bottles on display behind the bar. "Four fingers of Pennsylvania Highlander."

Placing two glasses on the counter, the bartender collected a half empty bottle of the nationally-famous whiskey and deftly decanted the required amount. While the price the man asked for the drinks caused a slight frown to come to Mansfield's face, being almost twice the normal sum, he raised no objection. Raising his glass and seeing that it looked to hold the full measure, he took a sip.

"What the—!" he began.

"Something up, feller?" the bartender demanded truculently.

"First drink at the end of the trail allus gets him that ways," Dusty replied before Mansfield could speak. "Let's go sit down a spell, Walt."

"What happened to it?" Mansfield demanded as they sat down at a table away from the bar. "I've never tasted anything so vile. Pennsylvania Highlander's usually real good stuff."

"That all depends how often the bottle's been filled, I reckon."

"You mean they water it down? Hell! No amount of water could make it taste this bad, and would show."

"Why sure," Dusty answered. "Only I'd bet this's not real Highlander. I'd say they emptied off and sold the real stuff then filled the bottle with some cheap slush brewed local."

"I paid for four fingers of Pennsylvania Highlander—!" Mansfield snorted.

"And got maybe three fingers of something

that costs the owner a whole heap less to buy," Dusty replied. "Drink her down and look at the glass."

Taking another sip, with an expression of distaste, Mansfield scowled. Although the four-finger glass appeared to hold its correct measure, the two small sips reduced its quantity in a surprising manner. With an effort he forced himself to empty the glass and studied it.

"Well I'll be damned!" he told Dusty. "I see now what you meant. Look at the thickness of the glass."

"I've seen it," Dusty assured him. "Only don't let the barkeeper know you have. We don't want any fuss yet, there's more to see."

"But I didn't get anywhere near the four fingers I paid for—"

"It's an old trick. Only in most places they wait until the feller's had a few drinks afore they pull it on him. I'd say the house makes a bottle in six out of the short measure from these glasses, but they make it look like he's getting all he pays for."

"Do all saloons do this?"

"Not all, General," Dusty replied. "And, like I said, most of 'em wait for the feller to get liquored afore they pull it. I don't like the way this feller did it so open. It looks like he reckons the local law'll back him if we raise fuss."

"Do we do it then?" Mansfield asked.

"Not yet," Dusty advised. "Like I said, there's more I want you to see. Let's get out of here and look around."

"How about the games?" Mansfield said.

"We can't tell much until they start running," Dusty replied. "I'd as soon we didn't let on we're nosing around."

"We'll go as soon as you've finished your drink," Mansfield stated and looked as Dusty rose with his glass untouched. "Aren't you going to drink it?"

"Nope," Dusty replied, taking a sip and coughing as if it bit his breath away.

"Maybe you'd best lay off that firewater until we've done some more doings, Sam," Mansfield suggested, taking his cue like a professional actor.

"It'd be best," Dusty answered as he set down the glass and stood up. As they walked across the room to the door, he went on, "Watch what the bartender does with my leavings."

Passing through the batwing doors, they came to a halt on the edge of the sidewalk.

Mansfield turned around in a casual manner and looked into the saloon. Slouching from his place, the bartender collected the glasses from the table. On his return to the counter, he uncorked the bottle and tipped the remains of Dusty's drink back into it.

"Well I'll be damned!" Mansfield growled.

"And me," Dusty admitted.

"Didn't you think he'd do that?"

"Nope. I reckoned he'd tip it into a bucket places like this keep behind the bar. Then at night they pour all they've gathered back into the bottles to be sold again the next day."

"The hell you say!" Mansfield ejaculated. "That stuff I just drank tasted like that's where it came from. How do you know about a game like that?"

"We caught a jasper at it in Quiet Town while I was marshal there," Dusty explained. "Made him drink two bottles of it afore we ran him out of town."

"What does liquor like that do to a man, Captain Fog?" Mansfield breathed, although his experiences in the Army gave him the answer.

"Gets him hog-wild, or so tangled that he wouldn't know a dime from a dollar—and fast."

46

"This could be just one isolated case," Mansfield remarked as they walked away from the saloon, but he did not sound convinced.

"We'll likely find out if it is, if we stay on to see," Dusty answered.

"How do you mean, if we stay on?"

"I tell you, General, I don't like the way this's going. Look at how the livery barn *hombre* acted for starters. Now this. If a bartender pulls a game like that with the glasses, and hardly lets us out of the place afore he pours an unfinished drink back into the bottle, it means he figures that he's real safe doing it. That says the local law'll back him all ways. Maybe we'd best call this off."

"For my sake?"

"Yep."

"I came here to get facts, Captain Fog. I've seen reasons for complaint and want to find out just how much more there is to it."

At that moment Dusty noticed the livery barn's owner step from an alley with a big, burly deputy marshal at his side. On spotting the small Texan and Mansfield, Sifter spoke softly to the deputy who gave them a long stare and nodded. Without giving a sign of it, Dusty studied the deputy and did not like what he saw. Dressed in range clothes, with a low hanging Colt on his right thigh, the man's appearance spelled hired hard-case to Dusty's west-wise eyes.

"Let's have something to eat, then take a look inside some of the stores," Mansfield suggested.

"There's an eating house along the street," Dusty replied. "May as well use it."

As they walked towards the café, Dusty noticed that Sifter was following them along the sidewalk, while the deputy kept pace with him across the street. Neither man entered the café, but were waiting when Dusty and Mansfield emerged after eating a good, if expensive, meal.

"That wasn't bad," Mansfield commented. "It cost high, but, like the woman said, they have to make their money while they can."

"No cowhand minds paying," Dusty pointed out. "It's how he's asked to pay and what he gets for his money that starts the fuss."

"That store across the street looks about the biggest, let's go look it over!"

"Sure. There's that barn owner and a deputy dogging our tracks, General."

"Why're they after us?" Mansfield asked without looking around.

"Could be weasel-face's suspic—" Dusty began. "Hey though! His eyes like to pop out of his skull when you flashed that roll of money. Could be they're looking for a way to lay hands on it."

"You mean take it by force?" Mansfield said. "I can hardly believe that, even if prices are high here."

"Maybe not by force, or by holding us up like Jesse James taking it from the railroad," Dusty admitted. "But they aim to have that money off us afore we leave town."

Before going into the store, Dusty and Mansfield stood looking at the goods displayed in its windows. Sifter walked by them without as much as a glance and entered the building. While pretending to be engrossed in the display, Dusty watched Sifter cross to the main counter and speak with the fat, well-dressed man behind it. Throwing a glance towards the window, the man nodded. Then he passed along the counter, showing a surprising turn of speed for one so bulky, turning over the price tags on the goods.

Instincts fined by years of riding trouble-torn trails sent a grim warning to the small Texan. Taken with the deputy watching from across the street, Sifter's actions in the store spelled danger. Unless he missed his guess, Dusty figured that General Mansfield would soon witness justice—Triblet style—in action.

Realizing that the affair must come to a boil sooner or later, Dusty decided to go ahead. So he raised no objections as Mansfield entered the store. Following his companion, Dusty glanced over his shoulder and saw the deputy crossing the street. On arrival, the man leaned against the store's door and looked inside as if waiting for something to happen.

It seemed that Mansfield did not lack powers of observation, for, on reaching the counter, he turned over the price tag on a pile of bandanas.

"I'll take one of these," he said, offering the storekeeper the lower of the prices he found inscribed on the card's two faces.

"It's twenty-five cents," the man objected.

"That's not what your sign here says," Mansfield pointed out.

"The sign's wrong. If you want that bandana, pay up. If you don't, put it down and stop mauling it."

"Maybe we should turn some more of them signs over, *amigo*," Dusty suggested.

"You keep your hands off them!" the

storekeeper spat out. "Are you in here to buy, or hunting trouble?"

"We figured on buying until we learned that you charge one price for Texans and another for townsfolks," Mansfield replied. "And those bandanas aren't worth even the ten cents you're asking the locals to pay."

Darting a glance at Sifter, the storekeeper leaned across the counter and laid a fat, greasy hand on the front of Mansfield's shirt.

"I don't take kind to being called a thief by a stinking beef-head," the man snarled and pushed with his hand.

Action and words proved to be a mistake. Mansfield had risen to the rank of brigadier general at a time when an officer's authority stemmed as much from his ability to enforce it physically as through the powers of the *Manual of Field Regulations*. Such a man would not mildly accept the kind of abuse handed out by the storekeeper. Already Mansfield had seen enough to tell him that, in Triblet at least, the Texans had justification for their complaints. Annoyed by the repeated cheating he had suffered since his arrival, the storekeeper's behaviour proved the last straw for Mansfield's temper.

Bracing himself, Mansfield resisted the

push and brought up his left hand to knock the man's hand from his chest. Then his bunched fist crashed into the fat face and the storekeeper sprawled backwards. Although Dusty knew that the attack was playing into Sifter's hands, it came too suddenly to be prevented.

"Hold it right there!" Sifter barked, drawing his Colt the moment Mansfield hit the storekeeper.

If Dusty needed further proof that their arrest was expected, the second deputy provided it. Even as Mansfield knocked the hand away, the man thrust open the door and entered. He came with his gun in hand, lining its barrel towards the counter and grinning in satisfaction.

While Dusty's speed on the draw would have allowed him to deal with Sifter, the other deputy's arrival prevented him from doing so. Before Dusty could turn from attending to Sifter, the second deputy would either cut him down or shoot Mansfield. So Dusty followed the sensible course by doing nothing. He figured that neither deputy regarded him as a serious factor. By keeping his true potential hidden, it would have a far more telling effect when produced at a more opportune moment.

"What's up, mister?" Dusty asked mildly, looking at Sifter.

"You're going to jail for disturbing the peace and assaulting this here tax-paying citizen," Sifter answered. "I figured you was trouble as soon as you rode in."

"You fix 'em good for what they done to me!" the storekeeper yelped, wiping the back of his hand across his mouth and looking at the red smear left on it.

"Trust us for that," the second deputy grinned, moving forward. "We don't go for beef-heads getting feisty in Triblet. Shed them gunbelts."

"Do it, General!" Dusty hissed.

Having spent considerable time on the range country, Mansfield could read the signs. Like Dusty, he knew that the deputy would not hesitate to shoot given half an excuse. So the General followed Dusty's lead in using the left hand to unbuckle and remove the gunbelt then drop it on the counter. Then he stood at the small Texan's side and awaited developments.

"What's going to happen to us, mister?" Dusty asked.

"That's for the judge to decide," Sifter answered, thrusting his face close to Mansfield's and sniffing. "They've been drinking, Rick."

"Smells that way," the other deputy answered. "I'd best go to the Lone Wolf and get the bottle to be used as evidence."

"I done it while they was eating," Sifter replied, taking a bottle of whiskey from his pocket, uncorking it and tossing some of the contents on to Mansfield's shirt.

"Try it!" grinned Rick, watching Mansfield tense.

Only by exerting all his will power did Mansfield hold himself in check. He stood still and watched Sifter spill more of the whiskey on to Dusty's clothes.

"Yes sir," Sifter grinned, corking and replacing the bottle. "They sure smell like they've tried to drink the Lone Wolf dry. Judge Rascover don't like drunks of any kind and fighting drunks least of all."

"Happen they don't cause us no fuss 'tween here and the jail house, he might let 'em off with a fine though," the other deputy went on. "And if they do make a fuss for us, I'm going to save the judge a heap of trouble."

"Will the judge give us a fair hearing?" Dusty asked.

"Fair as fair, runt," Rick answered. "Then he'll fine you for every red cent you've got and tell you to get the hell out of town."

Which was just about what Dusty expected to happen. So did Mansfield, if his expression was anything to go on. Dusty could see Mansfield savouring the shock he would hand to various Triblet citizens when he returned in his official capacity. Obeying the order to walk out and make for the jail, Dusty decided there would be no need to escape. After a mockery of a trial, the fine would be extracted and then their departure from town ordered and enforced. A faint grin twisted Dusty's face. General Mansfield had come to see for himself and the town of Triblet sure acted mightly co-operative in showing him plenty. However, Dusty concluded as they approached the marshal's office, they were safe enough as long as they kept their tempers—and Mansfield's true identity was not suspected.

Although the marshal's office proved to be empty when Sifter and Rick arrived with their prisoners, neither man seemed too surprised. Facing the main entrance, a door

55

opened to the rear of the building which housed the cells. From beyond it came the thud of blows and a hard, grating voice asking, "Where are they, damn you?"

"Looks like that feller in the cells ain't telling yet, Rick," Sifter remarked, nodding towards the door.

"I'll bet he does afore Kurt and the boys get through," the other deputy replied, crossing to the desk and putting the two gun-belts on it. "You pair stand there and keep your mouths shut, or I'll shut 'em with a gun barrel."

"Don't go talking like that to 'em, Rick," Sifter grinned as he went to the open door. "They might get scared and run."

"If they do, they can right easy be stopped," the other deputy answered, walking to the wall rack where he patted a Sharps Old Reliable rifle that towered over the Winchesters and shotguns. "Me and ole Lulu here've stopped escaping prisoners afore now with no sweat raised."

A thickset man in a well-cut town suit stood just inside the door, looking along the passage. As Sifter came up, the man turned towards him.

"We've brought those two beef-heads in

like you said, Judge," Sifter announced.

"I'll deal with them in a minute," the man answered, glancing to where Dusty and Mansfield stood by the desk and then swinging back to stare along the passage. "Is he ready to talk yet?"

"Not yet," answered the harsh voice. "Give him another in the guts, Lou."

A whooshing thud sounded, the noise a fist made when it drove into a man's stomach, followed by a moan of pain. Looking over the well-dressed man's shoulder, Sifter grinned and swung to glance back into the office. He saw the prisoners deep in conversation, speaking in such low tones that their words did not reach his ears.

"Dusty!" Mansfield whispered, after studying the flushed, side-whiskered face of the man in the passage. "I know that jasper!"

Realizing that only something urgent would make Mansfield forget the formal "Captain Fog", Dusty whispered back, "Will he recognize you?"

"Back in the War, I revoked his licence to act as a sutler in my command and impounded his goods for cheating the men. He'll recognize me all right."

In the Union Army, and to a lesser extent

among the blockade-starved Confederate troops, a camp sutler served as a source of supply for many items not issued by the Quartermaster Corps. Appointed by a State's Governor, or regimental or command officers, such men travelled with the soldiers and sold their wares for the highest possible prices. While some sutlers followed the rules laid down for their observance and contented themselves with a good, but—considering the risks involved—reasonable profit, others were outrageous profiteers. If a soldier owed a sutler money, the latter could attach up to a sixth of his pay until the debt was paid; a rule which caused much resentment. So a bad sutler could easily ruin a regiment or command's morale and a wise senior officer weeded the worst kind out.

However any man who invested heavily in such a venture—and the outlay went beyond purchasing a wagon, team and stock-in-trade, often entailing bribes to State or other officials to be granted the plum post—would not easily forget and forgive the cause of his losing the business.

With Mansfield's discovery, the whole situation had changed. No longer could he and Dusty rely on being fined and ordered out of town. As soon as Mansfield's identity became known, the judge and marshal would guess why he had gone to Triblet in such a manner. If they hoped to continue their activities in the town, Mansfield could not be allowed to leave.

Dusty figured the time had come when they must get the hell out of Triblet. Which raised the point of how to do it without having his or Mansfield's head blown off in the process.

"What're you pair whispering at?" Sifter demanded, advancing towards the desk with his revolver coming from its holster.

In the passage which fronted the cells, Judge Rascover tore his eyes from the sight of a man being brutally beaten by Marshal Kurt Magus and three deputies. Although he tried to shake it off, the feeling that he recognized one of Sifter's prisoners would not leave him. So he decided to take another look; not that he believed he had seen General Mansfield dressed as a Texas cowhand in the office.

"I was just telling my pard how welcome we'd been made in your sweet lil town," Dusty replied, watching Sifter come closer. "Why I do bet if you spent all the money you steal from us Texans on civic improvements,

Triplet'd make a good garbage dump."

"You've a big mouth for a runt!" Sifter spat menacingly.

"Big enough to spit in your face happen you come closer," Dusty answered.

"Why you—!" Sifter yelled, leaping forward and swinging around his revolver with the intention of slashing its barrel across Dusty's face.

Just an instant too late Sifter became aware of a change which seemed to come over Dusty. No longer did he look small and insignificant, but appeared in some way to take on size and heft until he dwarfed the man at his side.

Up flashed Dusty's hands, meeting, trapping and holding Sifter's arm as it drove at his face. At the same moment Dusty took a step to his right, pivoting on his left foot and heaving at the trapped limb. Using Sifter's momentum to aid his own far from inconsiderable strength, Dusty swung the man around in a half circle and released his hold. With a yell of surprise, Sifter shot forward, struck and went over the desk.

Coming to the door, Rascover stared at the men beyond the desk. His suspicion confirmed, he lunged through it and reached for the Colt

Storekeeper revolver in the vest holster under his jacket.

"Mansfi—!" he began.

Thrown over the desk, Sifter crashed into the Judge's legs before the word ended and brought him crashing to the floor. At the same moment a big, burly man with shoulder brown hair and long, drooping moustache appeared at the door to the cells. He wore a blood-smeared white shirt, string tie trailing unfastened from its open neck, trousers tucked into shining riding boots and a gunbelt sporting two ivory handled Army Colts butt forward in its holsters. Even without seeing the marshal's badge, Mansfield might have guessed he was Kurt Magus. Surprise twisted at Magus' face at what he saw, but he sent his bloody-knuckled right hand across to the left side revolver.

From pitching Sifter over the desk, Dusty whirled to deal with Rick. Although the deputy advanced to help Sifter, it was on Mansfield he directed his attention. The thought that Dusty might counter Sifter's attack so effectively never entered Rick's head, much less what the small Texan did next. Darting forward, Dusty bounded into the air. Rick held his revolver, but it lined on

61

Mansfield and Dusty's body went over its level. Even as Rick started to realize the danger, Dusty sent his feet lashing forward. Caught in the chest, Rick pitched backwards. The gun flew from his fingers as he landed on his back under the rifle rack.

Like many others who made the attempt, Sifter and Rick failed to understand the danger in trying to manhandle Dusty Fog. Their mistake might be considered excusable in that neither knew one very important detail. Down in the Rio Hondo a man called Tommy Okasi worked as Ole Devil Hardin's personal servant. Although many people thought him to be Chinese, Tommy came from the Japanese islands. He brought with him a thorough knowledge of his homeland's fighting arts. To Dusty, the smallest male member of the Hardin, Fog and Blaze clan, Tommy had taught the secrets of *ju-jitsu* and *karate*. The small Texan found the knowledge of leverage and making use of the other man's weight a great help when tangling with bigger, stronger attackers in a barehand brawl.

Much as Dusty's action surprised him, Mansfield did not stand idly by and watch. While satisfied that his companion had dealt with the immediate danger from Sifter and Rick, there were others ready to take a hand. Across the room, Magus was reaching for his gun and voices raised along the passage told that the disturbance in the office was bringing more men to investigate it.

Scooping up a large inkpot from the desk, Mansfield hurled it at Magus. With his Colt sliding from leather, the marshal saw the heavy missile flying towards his face and involuntarily jerked his head out of the way. Although he avoided being struck by the bottle, a spray of ink gushing from its open top splashed into his eyes. Half-blinded, he reeled away from the door without firing his Colt and blocked the path of the three deputies who ran from the cell where they had been helping to persuade a captured outlaw to give information.

Mansfield wasted no time in self-congratulation at having removed another threat to their safety. Instead he grabbed up the two gunbelts from the desk and swung around. He had not seen how Dusty dealt with Rick, but from all appearances the method had been successful and could be inquired about at a later more opportune moment.

"Let's get out of here!" he suggested,

thrusting Dusty's gunbelt into the other's hands.

"And *pronto*," Dusty agreed, heading for the front door.

Snarling curses, Magus lunged through the inner door as Dusty followed Mansfield on to the street. However Rascover, spitting out terms not usually employed by a leading light of the legal profession, chose that moment to thrust Sifter from him and stand up. In doing so he narrowly missed being shot, for Magus only just managed to retain his hold on the Colt's hammer and its barrel lined at the judge's back. Before Magus could spring to one side and take a fresh aim, the front door closed and his proposed victims ran along the sidewalk. Seeing them go by the window, Magus fired. His bullet shattered the glass, but missed the running men.

"Get 'em!" he screeched, ink-stained features contorted with rage. "Kill the bastards! Turn out every man in town to help if you have to!"

"Like hell!" Rascover yelped as the three deputies from the cells rushed by. "Hold it, you bunch!"

"What's up, Rasc?" Magus demanded indignantly, while his men came to a halt.

"We've got to get 'em. We can't let 'em get away—"

"You've never been righter!" Rascover answered. "That was Mansfield Sifter brought in."

"Who?" Magus snarled, glancing to where Sifter stood up.

"General Mansfield, the Governor of Kansas, that's who!" Rascover answered. "I'll never forget his lousy face and that was him."

"He looked like an ordinary Texas cowhand to me," Sifter protested.

"Which's how he wanted to be took!" Rascover spat back. "He must've come to Triblet to find out what goes on in a trail end town—"

"And he's done that!" Sifter said, bitterly recalling his treatment of the two men on their arrival. "We'll have to stop him getting away."

"But not with the townsfolk helping us," Rascover insisted. "Somebody else might recognize him and we don't want that."

"Take after 'em, Ed, Lou, Ben!" Magus ordered. "Tell everybody you see to leave 'em to us. If you can pin 'em down some

65

place, one of you come back and tell me as fast as you can."

"They'll be headed for my place and their hosses!" Sifter guessed. "If Elky hears shooting, he'll know what to do."

"See he hears some, Lou!" Magus shouted after the departing deputies.

"Sure," the tallest of the men replied and dashed out of the door holding his gun.

Three shots rang out on the street, telling that the deputies were following their orders. Then their footsteps sounded, drawing away from the building and they could be heard shouting for everybody to stay out of the way. If Rascover knew the citizens of Triblet, he felt sure they would be only too pleased to follow that advice.

"We'd best not waste time," Rascover told the others. "Mansfield'll likely have an escort close by ready to back him."

"Not closer than a mile off, I'll swear," Magus answered. "I thought you'd fixed it with one of his escort to let us know if he came this way."

"I thought I had, too," Rascover growled and looked to where a groaning Rick was dragging himself erect by the wall.

"Where they at?" Rick snarled thickly, glaring around. "I'll kill 'em."

"You'll likely get your chance at it," Rascover assured him.

"Maybe Mansfield pulled out without his escort knowing and just come with that one feller."

"Who the hell was he?" Sifter asked, rubbing his back. "He was as strong as a hoss and faster'n any man I've ever seen."

Through the broken window came the sound of shooting. First they heard the bark of a revolver mingled with the crack of a rifle, then two more revolver shots rang out.

"Down by your place, I'd say," Magus commented, looking at Sifter.

None of the men spoke for a moment, then Rascover said, "Somebody's coming."

Soon after the tallest of the three deputies entered. "Elky stopped 'em, but they holed up behind the water trough. That blond cuss's real fast and handy with his gun. Ben's watching 'em and Ed's warning folks to stay out of it."

"Let's go!" Magus barked. "Rick, take that Sharps up on the Lone Wolf's balcony and see if you can get a shot at 'em from there. Lou, take Ed up by Angie's hog-ranch. I'll be with Ben and you get into the barn, Sifter. Go up into the hay-loft. Wait until we're all in place afore you start shooting, Rick."

"Sure," the deputy answered, taking his Sharps rifle from the rack.

All the other deputies crossed to the rack, following Magus who selected a ten gauge shotgun. Sifter laid his faith in a Winchester while Lou collected a shotgun for himslf and a rifle to be used by his companion in the work ahead. Suddenly all became aware that no mention had been made of Judge Rascover's share in dealing with the escaped pair.

Realizing that he must show willing, but wanting to pick the part he played, Rascover thought fast. His first inclination was to suggest that he be left behind to guard the prisoner in the cells, but a split second's reflection told him the others would never agree to it. Knowing the identity of the man they were going after, Magus and his deputies would insist that everybody shared in the guilt. So Rascover proposed that he left by the rear door, circled around and came from the uncovered side of the barn. Magus threw a suspicious glance at him, but being aware that every second counted, raised no objections.

"Let's go get 'em," the marshal snarled and stalked on to the deserted street followed by his deputies.

Although he stood by the rack reaching for a rifle, Rascover did so only as a gesture of his good faith. With the others out of the building, he took his hand from the weapon and looked around. No matter which way the present business turned out, Rascover knew the old days in Triblet had ended. Even if Mansfield had left his escort without its members knowing his destination, he was certain to have taken precautions. Somebody he trusted would know where he had gone and what he planned to do. So his disappearance would bring men down to investigate. Once word of the "Texan's" identity came out, there were plenty of people around with grudges against Magus and Rascover just waiting for a chance to get even. So Rascover decided to leave while he could.

To travel and re-establish oneself called for money, which must be gathered before leaving. Unfortunately the office safe had two locks and Rascover possessed a key to only one. However he knew another place which held a large sum of money. With that thought in mind, he went out of the building's rear door.

Collecting a horse which stood saddled by the civic pound, he turned in the opposite direction to the livery barn and walked in the direction of the county land office.

When Dusty and Mansfield burst out of the marshal's office, the sight of their drawn revolvers sent the people walking or standing on the street leaping into shelter. Ignoring the bullet which smashed the office window as they went by, the two men ran along the street. Nobody opposed them, but Dusty suddenly became aware of something which might easily spoil their plans.

"Damn it!" he snapped. "The wind's changed right around."

Mansfield did not need to have explained what that meant. With the wind now blowing from the floating outfit's position to the town, the sound of shooting might not reach them. Glancing back, Mansfield saw three deputies dash from the office. One of the trio thumbed off three fast shots, but the bullets missed.

"They're after us!" Mansfield announced unnecessarily as the lead sang by their heads.

"Through the alley there then," Dusty replied, swerving across the street.

Coming from his store, after diving inside hurriedly as his victims approached, the man who had caused Dusty and Mansfield's arrest yelled to the deputies and offered his assistance. The words carried to the small Texan's ears, as did the reply that the local law could handle it themselves.

"That means they know for sure who you are and aim to have you dead," he told Mansfield. "They daren't have anybody else in the game in case you're recognized."

At the end of the alley they turned in the direction of the livery barn and headed towards it. Alert for danger, Dusty noticed that all the barn's doors had been closed, including the big doubled set at the front. Not quite all, he discovered as they drew closer. The small door cut into the front entrance stood open a crack. Even as Dusty became aware of that, he saw a rifle's barrel inching cautiously out of the opening and pointing in their direction.

"Behind the trough, General!" Dusty barked, bringing up his Colt, sighting and firing it all in one swift movement.

Swift-taken or not, the bullet flew to the desired place. Confident that he was an unsuspected element still, Elky received a sudden disillusionment. On hearing the shooting from the main street, he had followed his boss's instructions and had just completed closing the big doors when he saw the two men appear. So he caught up his rifle and prepared to drop at least one of the approaching pair. Looking along the Winchester's barrel, he waited for them to come so close that he could not miss.

With his finger squeezing the trigger, Elky saw Dusty's Colt-filled hand lift and point his way. Before the man could realize the danger and change his aim from Mansfield, he learned who formed the greater menace to him. Flame blossomed out of the Colt's barrel and a cloud of splinters erupted into his face from the side of the door. Pain caused him to jerk back and lift the barrel into the air just as he completed the trigger's rearward movement. The rifle bucked against Elky's shoulder, but its bullet flew harmlessly into the sky.

Having fired, Dusty followed Mansfield's leaping figure and dropped to his knees behind the water-trough.

"Did you get him?" Mansfield asked.

"I dunno, General," Dusty replied. "Here come the deputies."

"Damn it. I didn't want this to end in shooting."

"Or me, General, but the choice isn't in our hands," Dusty answered and threw two shots which caused the deputies to withdraw into the alley. "They've got us pinned down here and no way to reach the horses with that feller in the barn. So we're going to fight, or stay here permanent."

"Let's rush the barn and chance it," Mansfield suggested.

"It's too late, that feller's back. I must've only dusted his face with splinters. And there's a deputy in the alley with a clear shot at us if we go out."

"Only one?"

"The other two've pulled out, likely to get help."

"What'll Magus do?" Mansfield asked. "I'd say we're in a pretty good defensive position here. The water'll stop bullets from the front and those horses milling around in the corral make it difficult for anybody to draw a bead on us that way."

"It all depends on how well Magus knows his work," Dusty replied. "Was it me, I'd have a couple of men out by that house with the plank fence, get the cuss who arrested us up on the saloon balcony with his Sharps, send some help into the barn and to them houses across that side of it. Then I'd get with the deputy in the alley there and give them the signal to start shooting. That's how I'd handle it."

"Let's hope he's not that smart," Mansfield said grimly and looked across the range. "No sign of your boys yet."

"Likely they haven't heard the shooting," Dusty replied, starting to reload his Colt. "Could be we'll have to get out of this on our own, General."

After passing through the Lone Wolf's barroom without more than the words, "Magus sent me," to explain his presence to the owner, Rick carried his Sharp's rifle upstairs. A few customers and members of the staff watched them enter one of the front side first floor rooms, then began a soft-voiced discussion on the events they had just witnessed.

If aware of the interest he aroused, Rick gave no sign of it. He crossed to the room's window and let himself out on to the balcony. Then he moved along until he could look between the houses across the street at the water-trough. While he could not see either of his victims, he felt no concern. Designed for straight-shooting, hard-hitting work at long ranges, the Sharps' powerful bullets would tear great holes in the side of the trough and let the water out. Once empty, the wooden container would offer no further protection to the men concealed behind it.

Kneeling down, Rick rested the rifle's barrel on the balcony rail and took careful aim at the trough. A glance across the street told him that Magus was going along the alley to join the deputy already in it. Turning around, the marshal waved a hand towards the trough. Magus did not intend to wait until all his men reached their positions before beginning the work of emptying the trough.

With a cold, savage grin, Rick set his sights on the trough's centre plank and started to tighten his right forefinger on the trigger. The bellow of the Sharps' detonating powder charge came as something struck its barrel with vicious force. The unexpected impact tore the Sharps from Rick's hands, its wooden foregrip split open, and its bullet flew harmlessly off over the building across the street. To Rick's shocked ears came the distant crack of a Winchester. Although he grabbed for it with his numbed hands, the Sharps toppled over the balcony rail.

Lurching to his feet, mouthing curses and sending his right hand stabbing to the Colt at his thigh, Rick turned to discover who had dared to intervene. He saw a tall, slim figure dressed in all black Texas range clothing tearing along the street afork a magnificent white stallion and holding a still-smoking Winchester rifle. Despite the anger he felt at the damage to and loss of his rifle, Rick could still think objectively. Any man who could make a hit on the barrel of the Sharps along that length of street possessed considerable skill in the use of a Winchester. Too much to be taken on when armed only with a Colt revolver. So Rick put aside any thought of drawing and shooting from the balcony. Turning, he darted to the window from which he had emerged and climbed through it. After quickly working the throb from his fingers, he drew the Colt, crossed the room, opened the door and stepped cautiously on to the inside balcony which overlooked the bar.

Crouched in cover which looked hardly large enough to conceal a jack rabbit, the Kid had watched Dusty and Mansfield's flight from the jail. For a moment he paused, but the sight of deputies following told him his help would be needed. Turning, he gave a piercing whistle and his white stallion appeared from a hollow a quarter of a mile away. The horse loped to its master and he swung into the saddle, bending to slide the Winchester from its boot.

"It's sure lucky the wind changed just now, Nigger hoss," the Kid said with a grin as he started to ride towards the town.

By the time the Kid reached the end of the street, it lay as empty as Death Valley on a hot summer noon. Eagle-keen eyes raked the street as the white walked forward. The flurry of shooting at the livery barn told the Kid where to find Dusty but he rode with the caution of a Comanche Dog Soldier on a raiding trail. At first he saw nothing to disturb him, then his eyes picked up Rick's Sharps as it rested on the saloon's balcony rail.

Having worked as a deputy under Dusty Fog, the Kid knew instantly what the Sharps meant. He could see no sign of its user, but knew the other must be stopped shooting. A touch of the heels brought the white stallion to an instant halt and the Winchester rose smoothly to the Kid's shoulder. Taking careful sight on the slender mark offered by the Sharps' barrel, he gently caressed the Winchester's delicate set-trigger. Forty grains of powder burned and a flat-nosed bullet sped on its way, flying true to bat the Sharps from its unsuspecting owner's hands.

Satisfied with the result of his shot, the Kid again nudged his stallion in a gentle signal. From standing like a statue, the big horse broke into a racing stride and carried its rider towards the Lone Wolf Saloon. Seeing Rick's jack-in-a-box appearance and hurried departure, the Kid followed his intentions as if he carried them inscribed on a banner above his head. As he drew near to the saloon, the dark youngster swung his right leg up and sat as if riding a fancy dude side-saddle. Then he launched himself from the horse's back, landed on the hitching rail and sprang from there to the sidewalk.

Along with the other occupants of the saloon, the bartender who had served Dusty and Mansfield stood at the front windows to watch what happened. At the sight of the Sharps falling from above, he saw a chance for advancement in Triblet's society. Although being a bartender paid well, the post of deputy marshal offered greater remuneration for less work. So, aware that opportunity knocked only once, he decided to take a hand in the game. With that thought in mind, he forced himself back through the other on-lookers, ran to the batwing doors and charged through with his Colt ready for use in defence of Triblet, home and beauty.

The bartender failed to realize just how close the Kid was until too late. When the man appeared, the dark youngster wasted no time in debating whether he be friend or enemy. He held the Winchester in his right hand only, using the left to help retain his balance as he lit down on the sidewalk, but it proved to be enough. Swinging his right arm as the bartender started to turn his way, he sliced his rifle up. The octagonal-shaped barrel caught the man in the throat with considerable force, spun him around and sent him stumbling back through the doors.

Rick saw the bartender leave as he reached the head of the stairs. When the other returned so promptly, the deputy could not prevent himself from jerking up and firing his revolver. Fortunately for the bartender, who had problems enough merely trying to breathe at that moment, he was already falling as he entered and the bullet ploughed into the doors above him.

Shooting proved to be an error of tactics for Rick, as the sound told the Kid the location of at least one enemy. Again the doors flew open inwards. Bounding over the bartender's body, the Kid leapt into the barroom with his rifle already slanting upwards.

Shock bit into Rick as he thumbed back the Colt's hammer and desperately tried to line its barrel on the fast-moving figure below. As he came to a halt, the Kid had completed his aiming. A touch on the trigger and the Winchester cracked. Muzzle-blast flared from the rifle's barrel and Rick pitched backwards as its bullet tore into his chest. Hitting the wall, the deputy rebounded from it. His Colt fell from a limp hand. Striking the flimsy balcony, Rick's weight broke it and he crashed to the floor in front of the bar.

With the Winchester's lever blurring to eject the empty case and replace it by a loaded bullet, the Kid swung to face the occupants of the room. Smoothly, almost casually, the rifle's barrel made an arc which seemed to encompass every man present. That, taken with the Comanche-mean, Indian-dark face—which no longer gave the slightest impression of youth or innocence—proved sufficient to end all movement.

"Any more of 'em up there?" the Kid demanded.

"Just him, feller," a man replied.

From his clothing and general air of authority, the Kid judged the speaker to be either the floor manager or owner of the saloon. In an effortless movement, the rifle turned and spat. A bottle standing on a table burst under the impact of the bullet. Again the lever made its flickering arc and an empty case somersaulted through the air to clink on to the floor.

"Anybody taking it up for him?" the Kid inquired and the rifle's muzzle turned until it pointed at the big mirror behind the bar.

"Not in here there ain't!" the spokesman declared vehemently, guessing what the Kid had in mind and wishing to avoid damage to his fixtures. "I'll see to that."

"Be right obliged if you would," drawled the Kid and headed for the stairs. He could hear more shooting outside and knew that his help might still be needed.

Nobody moved or spoke until after the dark young Texan disappeared into one of the upstairs rooms. Then a grizzled, bearded railroad engineer, veteran of many trail end towns, spat with accuracy into a spitoon and looked around.

"Something tells me this here town's due for a clean up," he announced with tones of satisfaction. "That, gents, was the Ysabel Kid and you can bet that where he is, the rest of the floating outfit ain't far behind."

Making his way from cover to cover, Mark Counter approached the house with the high plank fence around it. He had seen Dusty and Mansfield arrive at the livery barn and knew his help would be needed. Still he kept in cover, meaning to appear unexpectedly on the scene and throw in his weight where it would do most good. From all he could see, passing down the rear of the line of houses offered the best way to reach an advantageous position.

On reaching the fence, he moved along it and peered cautiously around the end. Seeing the two deputies appear from between two of the buildings further along, he withdrew his head again. As they had been looking towards the livery barn, Ed and Lou failed to notice Mark's brief appearance. Short it might have been, but the blond giant saw all he needed to while making it.

Aided by considerable experience in fighting, Mark instinctively dissected the matter and drew his conclusions. To step out immediately and confront the men would be no answer. There was no chance that they might mistake him for a harmless visitor. Any Texan would be suspect and treated as an enemy under the circumstances. While very good with his matched Colts, the shotgun and rifle in the deputies' hands nullified Mark's advantage at that distance. Nor could he go around the front of the fence without exposing himself to the rifle in the barn. Mark knew his only chance was if he could somehow take the two men by surprise, get the drop on them before they could bring their weapons into use.

Gripping the top of the fence, Mark drew himself up and rolled over. He dropped into the grounds of a fair-sized house and stood for a moment looking around. Whoever owned the place appeared to care little for gardening as only uncut grass grew around the house. That did not interest Mark, whose main interest rested on the possibility of taking the two deputies by surprise. From what he could see, there was only one gate in the fence.

"The damned thing would be on the front side," Mark mused, bitterly aware that going out through it would put him in full view of the rifleman in the livery barn. "I'll just have to hope there's a way out I can't see for the house."

Starting forward, he directed his steps towards the rear of the building. So far he could see no sign of life from it, which did not surprise him. Either the occupants could not hear the shooting, or were wisely remaining indoors to keep out of the way of stray bullets. If there should be a gate hidden by the house, he might still achieve his intentions.

A clothesline draped with a quantity of assorted female underclothing stretched from the house to a pole standing against the fence. Glancing at the various garments hanging exposed to his view, Mark grinned and ducked underneath. Then his face lost the grin, for he heard the deputies approaching beyond the fence. At the same moment a pretty blonde girl wearing a fancy kimono and very little else walked around the corner of the house. She carried an armful of freshly-washed clothes, meaning to hang them on the line. Coming to a halt, she stared at the big

Texan with a mixture of appraisal, interest and annoyance.

"What're you doing here?" she demanded. "We ain't open yet, and Angie don't take kind to fellers sneaking around the back here peeking on us."

"Damned if it's not an instinct born into us Counters to find these places," Mark thought, realizing the nature of the business carried out in the building.

"You get out of he—!" the girl went on, her voice rising.

The words ended and she dropped the clothes as Mark took a step in her direction. Realizing that the girl's voice might reach the deputies, Mark acted fast. Before she could scream, he scooped her into his arms and started to kiss her. At first she struggled, beating at his shoulders with her fists and trying to drive her knee into his groin. Before the knee reached its target, her hands stopped flailing and her arms crept around Mark's neck as she responded to his kiss. On being released, she staggered back a couple of steps unmindful of the washing beneath her feet. Leaning against the wall of the house, eyes glassy and mouth trailing open, she raised no further objections to the blond giant's presence.

Voices drifted to Mark's ears from beyond the fence, warning that the deputies were going by.

"Pity we ain't got time to call in on Angie, Ed," said one of them. "She's got a new gal with apples like cannonballs."

"You'll not get a chance to suck at 'em happen we don't get Mansfield and that Texan," the second speaker warned grimly. "They've seen enough to run us clear out of this town."

Gauging their whereabouts by the sound of their voices, Mark prepared to deal with the deputies. A simple way of taking them by surprise leapt to his mind, although not one which would occur to everybody.

After one more glance at the girl, whose kimono hung open and left little to be imagined Mark concluded that she might be the one mentioned by the deputy. Putting the thought from his head, he swung away from her and crossed the garden at a run. Down dropped his left shoulder and he hurled himself at the fence. Under the impact of Mark's one hundred and ninety pound, bone-tough frame, the planks crackled and burst outwards.

Going through the shattered section of the fence, Mark crashed into Ed and sent him sprawling backwards. Although Lou avoided being struck by either his pard or Mark, the blond giant's dramatic appearance so shocked him that he just stood and stared.

Not for long.

Before the deputy could recover from his surprise, Mark lashed around a backhand slap. Caught at the side of the head, Lou formed a momentary idea that a mule had kicked him. The force of the blow flung him several feet in a spinning sprawl to plough up dirt with his chin, but he did not feel his landing, or anything else for some time to come.

Catching his balance with an effort, Ed came to a halt. He still held the rifle in his left hand and grabbed at the wrist of the butt with his right. By the house, the girl stared with amazement through the ruined fence. She saw the deputy start to swing the rifle into line on Mark and screamed a warning.

"Behind you, mister!"

Although welcome, the warning had not been entirely necessary. Mark knew that the collision had not put the first man out of the game and was already moving to deal with him. As the blond giant swung to face Ed, his right hand dipped gun-wards. All in a single, lightning fast, yet effortless appearing move, Mark slid the off side Colt from its holster and fired. A bullet spun through the rifling of the seven and a half inch barrel to churn its way into Ed's chest. Reeling under the blow from the heavy bullet, the deputy flung aside his rifle and collapsed by the shattered section of the wall.

Turning again, the Colt cocked on its recoil and ready for use, Mark glanced at Lou. From all appearances, the deputy could be discounted as an active participant in the fight. Then Mark looked at the girl and nodded his head gratefully.

"Thanks, honey," he said before turning his attention to the two men and half-a-dozen or so girls who came out of the house. "You folks'd best get inside again. Could be there'll be more lead flying around here."

Showing the speed of decision and sound common sense life in wild frontier towns encouraged, the party returned to the house. Civic loyalty and public duty might require that they investigated, or offered their assistance to the local peace officers but none felt inclined to do so. Magus and his men demanded too much in bribes and service to be popular among the citizens, especially those whose business, while necessary, was termed illegal. Only the blonde remained outside and she walked across the garden to the gap in the fence.

"What'll happen to me when they come to, mister?" she asked. "They'll want my hide for warning you."

"I wouldn't let that worry me, was I you," Mark replied. "With any luck, their term of office just ended."

"Then how's about you and me going in for a cup of java?" the girl inquired. "Angie won't mind."

"I wish I'd time right now, honey," Mark told her. "You keep the pot boiling for a spell and I'll be back to try your—coffee."

"I'll be waiting," she promised. "And it won't cost you a dime." Watching Mark walk away, she hugged her torso with her arms and sighed. "Big feller," she breathed. "It'll be a real pleasure."

Like Mark Counter, Doc Leroy approached Triblet on foot. Coming in from the opposite side to the blond giant, Doc intended to visit the jail and attend to any deputies it might hold before joining the others at the livery barn. A faint grin twisted at Doc's lips as he wondered what Dusty would make of the floating outfit's timely arrival. Under the circumstances, he doubted whether the small Texan was likely to complain about the slight improvement the others had made to the plan of operations.

"Anyways," Doc told himself philosophically, "Lon, the boy and me can always lay the blame on Ma—"

Something he saw ahead of him drove all thoughts of laying blame on Mark from Doc's head. Coming to a halt, he looked at the rear of the main street's buildings. The sight of Judge Rascover leaving a saddled horse and entering the back door of a building brought a change to Doc's plans. Finding Rascover alone presented an attractive possibility to Doc's fertile mind. Given suitable inducement—say the nose of a .45 Peacemaker gouging into his backbone—the judge might feel it his bounden duty to advise the citizens that they should not help the peace officers. Anyways, Doc figured it worth trying and so made for the building. Looking to one side, he saw the Kid riding towards the town.

"Trust that danged Comanche to pick the chore where he could do it all on the back of his horse," Doc thought indignantly. "This walking's plumb hell on the feet!"

With that, Doc drew his Colt and walked up to the building. Easing open the door, he stepped through cautiously. He found himself standing in a passage which led to the front of the building and had two doors on either side. One of the doors was open and from beyond it came a familiar-sounding "thwack!" followed by a heavier thump.

Advancing silently, Doc peered around the edge of the door. He found that his guess at the cause of the sounds—somebody receiving a blow on the head and collapsing to the floor—was correct. A small man in his shirt-sleeves sprawled face down while Rascover, revolver in hand, was approaching the open safe by the desk under the window. Just as Doc prepared to enter the room, another thought struck him. If the citizens of Triblet learned their judge had been robbing them, they would be far less inclined to support the local law. So Doc waited until Rascover had stuffed a fair sum of money into his pocket, using the left hand and still keeping the Colt in his right fist, before announcing his presence.

"Throw the gun across the room and turn slow, your dishonour," he said.

Tensing at the first word, Rascover retained sufficient self control to avoid acting rashly. Slowly he twisted his torso around until he could look over his shoulder at the speaker. To somebody unversed in such matters, Doc might have appeared mild, studious of features, innocuous almost. Rascover did not think so. Taking in the casual, competent ease with which the Colt was lined on him, he read Doc's true potential and knew better than to take chances.

"What's this?" Rascover demanded.

"I never knew that this's how a judge gets paid," Doc replied, stepping forward. "The gun, your dishonour."

"What about it?"

"It's still in your hand, not lying across there in the corner of the room like it should be."

"I don't know what you mean, young man," Rascover announced in his most impressive judicial manner. "I just came here—"

"To draw your retirement pension, I'd say," Doc finished for him. "Only I don't reckon the folks around town'd call it that."

A point with which Rascover heartily concurred, although he failed to mention the fact. Nor did he offer to turn and try to use his gun.

"I suppose you know that it's against the law to throw down on a respected member of the bar?" he asked, playing for time.

"Do tell," Doc drawled, then his voice hardened. "It'll be more than just throwing down on you if that gun's not across in the far corner *pronto*."

If Rascover had no legal right to the title he bore, he could claim to be a real good judge of human nature. So he knew that he had pushed the matter as far as possible without taking it to the ultimate conclusion of throwing lead. Knowing what the end result of that would be, unless the situation radically changed in his favour, he decided to obey. With a shrug, he tossed his revolver across the room.

"You could get into serious trouble over this," he warned. "I'm not without in-fluence—"

"You're a robbing skunk and we both know it," Doc interrupted.

"There's a fair pile of money in the safe here—" Rascover hinted.

"Yep," agreed Doc. "Only there sure wouldn't've been if I hadn't come in."

At that moment the man on the floor moaned and stirred. Despite never having completed his studies and qualified, Doc possessed the instincts of a doctor, even though he occasionally found himself forced to forget certain parts of the Hippocratic oath. So he gave the man his attention. Rascover's gun lay at the far side of the room and he did not appear to be carrying any other weapon. Figuring he could draw his Colt before the Judge reached the discarded revolver, Doc slipped it back into the holster. Dropping to one knee, the slim cowhand turned his eyes from Rascover to the Judge's victim. One glance told Doc that the man had sustained no serious damage and ought to be in full control of his faculties very shortly. So it proved. Shaking his head and groaning a little, the man turned himself into a sitting position. He glared around in a dazed manner until his eyes came to rest on Rascover standing before the safe.

"You whomped me on my head!" the man screeched, raising a hand to touch the lump on his skull. "I allus knowed you was a crook, Ras—Watch him, Texas!"

One quick look as Doc holstered the Colt told Rascover the futility of trying to reach his own gun. However a second weapon, as yet unsuspected by the slim Texan, lay closer to hand. Inside the safe was a Remington Double Derringer, left there to be used in case the chance presented itself during a hold-up. Slowly Rascover lowered his right hand, trying to keep it hidden by his body. Just as his fingers closed on the Derringer's butt, he heard the clerk's accusing words.

Spitting out a most un-legal oath, Rascover raised the gun and started to whirl around. Like a flash Doc lunged upright. While he was still straightening up, his right hand flickered and the ivory handled Colt seemed to meet it in midair. Having drawn back the hammer and depressed the trigger while the Colt was clearing the holster, he held it ready to fire with the minimal waste of time. Merely raising his thumb allowed the hammer to swing forward and drive its striker against the base of the waiting cartridge.

Almost turned towards Doc, Rascover saw

95

that he would be too late. The Colt in the Texan's almost boneless looking hand roared. A screech broke from Rascover as the bullet knifed into his shoulder. At that he might have counted himself fortunate, for Doc had not aimed to make such a hit but merely to prevent the other from shooting. The Derringer clattered from Rascover's limp fingers and he fell backwards against the safe.

"You should've blowed the robbing son-of-a-bitch's head off, friend," yelped the clerk, rising to his feet and staggering.

"Easy on there," Doc warned, shooting out his left hand to steady the man.

"Agh!" Rascover moaned, clutching at his shoulder and sinking to his knees. "I'm hurt bad. Get the doctor."

"He left town this morning and won't be back all day," the clerk replied with a certain amount of relish. "Likely you'll bleed to death afore he gets here."

At which point Rascover finally recognized Doc. With its reputation for salty toughness and ability to protect its own, the Wedge had suffered less than most other trail crews during its visit to Triblet. However, the local doctor being away on a house call to a distant ranch, Doc had been requested to remove a bullet from a man shot in a quarrel over a card game. Remembering the skilled manner in which the pallid young man had performed the operation, and the town's doctor's praise-filled comments later, Rascover saw a chance of saving himself from the fate suggested by the clerk.

"Help me, Leroy!" Rascover moaned.

"Why should I?" Doc asked.

"I—I'll give you anything—"

"You don't have anything," Doc pointed out.

"Please help me!" Rascover whined, grovelling across the floor on his knees towards Doc.

"Allus figured he'd show yeller give the chance," the clerk commented. "Hey! Listen to all that shooting. What's coming off?"

"It's house-cleaning time," Doc explained, once more holstering his Colt. "General Mansfield brought Cap'n Dusty Fog in to help do it."

"And not afore time," the clerk growled. "Reckon they'll need any help?"

"Will they, your dishonour?" asked Doc.

"M-Magus and the deputies went after 'em," Rascover answered. "I didn't want him to, but he wouldn't listen—"

"He's a liar as well as a thief," the clerk spat out.

"For God's sake help me!" Rascover pleaded. "I'll do anything you ask, tell you anything you want to know, but help me!"

"Get on your feet," Doc ordered. "Come on, get up. I can't do a son-of-a-bitching thing for you here and I don't aim to tote you to the doctor's house if you faint away."

"And I sure as hell won't," the clerk went on. "If he don't walk, leave him to bleed to death, friend."

"I might just do that," Doc threatened.

Lurching to his feet, Rascover stumbled out of the room followed by Doc and the clerk. People had gathered in the street and many faces turned Rascover's way as he appeared at the door of the county land office. At another time the Judge might have called on the citizens to help him, or accused Doc of robbing the safe. With the throbbing pain in his shoulder acting as a reminder, the idea never occurred to him. Instead he was willing to say anything the Texan wanted if doing so would hasten the attention to his wound.

"Tell 'em everything that happened in there," Doc ordered as several people ran towards them. "And let 'em know who Magus and his bunch're trying to kill."

Making his way vigilantly towards the livery barn, Waco saw its owner—although he did not recognize Sifter as such—approaching from the other direction. At the sight of the deputy's badge on Sifter's vest and the rifle in his hand, Waco flattened himself behind the thick trunk of the old cottonwood tree. Clearly the other man did not suspect the youngster's presence, for he walked straight up to the barn's rear door and entered.

There had been a time when Waco would have acted in a different manner and stepped out to face the man disregarding the fact that the distance separating them favoured the other's rifle. Early in his association with Dusty Fog, the youngster had learned to think first instead of charging blindly forward behind a smoking Colt.

During the time Waco served as one of Dusty's deputies in Mulrooney, he had received a thorough grounding in practical law enforcement. So he knew why Sifter was entering the barn. Such a building would store its hay in a loft above the stalls. Once that jasper climbed into the loft, he could see the rear of the water-trough and take the necessary action against the men it concealed.

From what Waco could see and hear, the affair was rapidly coming to a full boil. There would be no time for finesse, or long thought to decide how he must act. He walked towards the side of the barn and there was no door in it. However it offered a choice of two windows as a means of making an entrance.

"Sure hope the owner don't mind me busting through one of 'em," he breathed. "Anyways, I can allus say Mark told me to do it."

Taking comfort in that thought, the youngster drew both his matched Colts and launched himself forward. Covering his head with his arms, Waco dived at the window at the front end of the building. He broke through to the accompaniment of clashing, broken glass and shattered framework. While falling to the floor, he saw Sifter at the foot of the ladder leading to the hay-loft. As Waco lit down, rolling like he had taken a toss from a bad horse, Sifter twisted to face him and swung the rifle in his direction. Lead screamed over Waco as he continued to roll. While still on his back, he extended the right hand Colt at arm's length above his head, took rapid aim and fired.

Sifter flinched as the bullet made its eerie slapping sound by his ear in passing and worked the Winchester's lever. Trained as a peace officer by a man who knew the work, Waco did not hesitate to carry defending his life to the ultimate conclusion when necessary. He knew it to be necessary at that moment, for Sifter intended to kill him. Still rolling, he cut loose with his left hand Colt as he landed on his stomach. Shooting from such a position allowed him to take a better aim, as he proceeded to demonstrate. He shot the only way he dare under the circumstances, to make an instant kill before the other drove lead into him. Directed at Sifter's head, the bullet glanced off the rifle's barrel and twisted in the air. It struck between the man's eyes sideways on. Flung backwards, Sifter dropped the rifle, hit the ladder and bounced from it to fall face down. The back of his skull appeared to have been torn open from the inside.

At which point Waco became aware of a second man's presence in the barn. One thing saved the youngster's life. Although Elky had heard the sound of his arrival, he believed

101

Sifter could deal with the newcomer. When the Colt fired its second shot without an answering crack from the owner's rifle, Elky realized that he had called the turn wrongly. He also knew that he must do something—and fast.

With that intention Elky began to swing his rifle around. In his haste he failed to withdraw it fully from the opening through which he had been bombarding the water trough. The barrel struck the side of the door and knocked it open, then came free and continued to turn in Waco's direction.

Behind the water trough, Mansfield saw the top of the small door jerk inwards. Curiosity caused him to chance a bullet and take a closer look. He saw Elky turn and line the rifle at somebody inside the barn. That somebody could only be a friend, one of the floating outfit. Judging by the sounds of shooting from inside the building, whoever it was probably had his hands full enough without Elky adding to his problems. Swiftly Mansfield brought up his Remington, resting his wrist on the edge of the trough and laying his sights without a thought of being exposed to Magus and the deputy in the alley's fire.

Guessing what Mansfield was trying to do,

Dusty also came up and his Colt cracked twice. Magus ducked back into the alley as a bullet fanned his face and Ben wavered between the two targets offered. Before the deputy reached a decision, the Remington barked and Mansfield dropped behind the walls of the trough once more. An instant later Dusty joined in.

With the barrel of the rifle slanting down towards Waco, and right forefinger squeezing its trigger, Elky saw the youngster trying to turn his way. Then something which burned like a red-hot iron gouged into the man's shoulder from behind. Shock and pain thrust Elky forward, his rifle banging as he went. The bullet struck the floor ahead of Waco, flinging a spray of dirt against his chest. Rolling over the depression caused by the lead, he lined his right hand Colt in Elky's direction.

"Don't shoot!" the man screeched, dropping his rifle and sinking to his knees. "I'm done!"

Alert for treachery, Waco rose to his feet. At no time did he take his Colt out of line or present Elky with a chance to make a hostile move. Holstering his left hand gun, he walked across to the groaning man's side.

Elky knelt on the floor, face twisted in pain and tried to reach around his torso with the left hand in an attempt to stop the blood flowing from his wound. With the deft skill of a trained lawman, the youngster plucked the revolver from Ekly's holster and hurled it into the hay-loft. Picking up the rifle, Waco stepped by the man and looked cautiously out of the door. From what he saw, he concluded that the fight was rapidly approaching its climax and he waited to see how he could next help his friends.

"They've arrived!" Mansfield breathed, ducking back behind the trough after saving Waco's life. "That was fast work."

"Real fast," Dusty answered dryly, setting his Colt's hammer at half cock and resting its butt on his knee.

"What now?" Mansfield inquired.

While pumping the empty cases from the cylinder's chambers and replacing them with bullets from his belt loops, Dusty looked around. He saw the saloon's balcony had been vacated by Rick and turned his eyes towards the open range. Stepping briefly into view from behind the plank fence surrounding Angie's brothel, Mark gave Dusty a cheery hand-wave which said all was well in that direction. Waco's presence in the barn, taken with the lack of further shooting, meant there would be no more opposition from that side. If Dusty knew the Kid and Doc, he expected them to be dominating the main street and keeping back any possible reinforcements for the local law.

"I'd say it was time to settle with Magus," the small Texan stated, completing the loading of his Colt. "So I'll go over and do it."

"Don't let him wearing a badge worry you, Dusty," Mansfield said grimly. "You take him any way you have to."

"That's just what I aimed to do," Dusty answered in the quiet tone the OD Connected hands rarely heard yet knew so well.

When Dusty Fog spoke in that manner, it was time to hunt for the storm shelters. Watching the grim set of the *big* Texan's face, Mansfield knew that Dusty or Magus would be dead very soon unless the marshal surrendered.

Then Dusty did something which came as a complete surprise to Mansfield. Raising his voice, the small Texan yelled, "Waco!"

"Yo!" came the old cavalry response from inside the barn.

"Get across to the right side," Dusty shouted in a voice which reached the ears of the men in the alley. "I'm going after them when you yell."

"It's done!" Waco yelled back.

Before the words ended, or Mansfield could remonstrate with him for his apparent folly in advertising his plans to the enemy, Dusty moved. He sprang from behind the trough like a sprinter in a foot-race leaving the starting line. Everything depended on Magus and the deputy acting in the required manner.

Having heard Dusty's shouted instructions, Magus and Ben behaved just as he hoped they would by turning their attention towards the barn. Catching sight of the small Texan erupting from cover out of the corner of his eye, Magus tried to swing around. In doing so, he pressed the shotgun's trigger an instant too soon. Dusty heard the wicked boom of the gun and the whistle of a close-passing buck-shot ball, but was outside the deadly pattern of the load. Nor did Ben fare any better with his revolver against the racing figure. Before Magus could bring the shotgun down from its recoil kick, Dusty had reached the edge of the corral.

Spooked by the shooting, the horses milled around and churned up the earth in swirling clouds of dust. Ducking between the rails, Dusty rose and tried to see across the corral. While the dust all but hid Magus and the deputy, and the constant movement of the horses prevented Dusty from aiming his revolver at them, he realized they were in no better position. With that thought in mind, Dusty looked around for a means to reach and deal with the men.

"They've got help!" the deputy at Magus' side snarled.

"So've we!" the marshal replied, but his voice lacked conviction. "Watch that short cuss, he's in the corral someplace."

"Just let him try to come out!" Ben growled.

In the barn, Waco followed Dusty's plan without needing any verbal amplifications. So he darted across to the side window and, as he approached it, studied the situation. That shotgun would be a deadly menace when Dusty emerged from the corral, so it must be taken out of the game. Doing so without catching nine buckshot balls in the process called for thought. Swiftly Waco applied the thought and came up with what he regarded as the answer. Raising Elky's rifle, the youngster hurled it out of the window.

Still expecting something to happen from that direction, Magus swivelled around as the window broke. Seeing the man turn the shotgun his way, Waco leapt sideways. The shotgun bellowed from across the alley and nine splinter-raising holes burst in the planks just ahead of where the youngster had come to a halt.

"Now there's a close-patterning gun," Waco remarked, studying the damage as he sprang once more towards the window.

Dusty moved half-crouching through the swirling dust of the corral. As a horse brushed by him, he sought for another animal noticed earlier. It came into view, a big, powerful bay with lines that told of speed and agility. Before the bay reached him, Dusty holstered his Colt. He heard the boom of Magus' shotgun and guessed that Waco had managed to draw the marshal's fire. There was no time to waste and Magus must not be allowed to reload the gun. While willing to risk the two men's revolvers, Dusty knew he stood no chance at all against the shotgun at close quarters.

As the bay drew near, Dusty ran to meet it. Catching hold of its mane, he vaulted on to its back. A moment to gain some semblance of control over the startled horse and he sent it towards the side of the corral. From his place on the bay's back, Dusty was above the worst of the dust. He saw Magus drop the shotgun and turn to run, but Ben was still facing the corral. Then Dusty had to devote his full attention to controlling the horse. Left to its own devices, the bay would not have thought to try leaping the gate. However it responded to Dusty's guidance and showed no sign of flinching as the fence drew closer. The gate, lowest part of the enclosure, faced the mouth of the alley, an unfortunate fact which Dusty accepted as being unavoidable. At no other point could the bay be expected to leap high enough to carry them over the rails.

Whoever owned and trained the horse knew his work. Dusty could feel it gathering itself and the powerful muscles bunching for the effort. Then it rose into the air, carrying him up and over the top rail of the gate as sweetly as he could have wished it to be done.

In the alley, Ben saw Dusty approaching and brought up his revolver. With his left hand supporting the right, the deputy started to take aim. The thought of who he was dealing with caused Ben to waste valuable seconds instead of starting to shoot at the first sight of the small Texan. Figuring that a miss would be fatal, he gripped the gun and prepared to take Dusty at the moment when the other could do least about protecting himself.

With all his attention focussed on controlling the horse and staying on its bare back, Dusty could do nothing to defend himself against the deputy. Two of his friends saw the danger and were in a position to do something about it. Up on the balcony at the Lone Wolf, the Kid changed his aim from the fleeing Magus. Cold red-hazel eyes glinted along the Winchester's barrel and sent a message to the finger on the trigger. At the same moment Waco appeared at the livery barn's window and his Colt barked. Two bullets, either of which would have been fatal, tore into Ben. Flung into the wall of the nearer building, the revolver falling unfired from his hands, the deputy went down.

Only Dusty's superb riding skill kept him on the bay's back as it landed from leaping over the gate. Deft hands and legs steadied the horse, helping it to maintain its balance and recover from the jump. On landing, Dusty urged his mount along the alley after the fleeing marshal.

Hearing the approaching rumble of hooves, Magus looked back to learn who was following. Fury lashed at the marshal as he found his pursuer to be the man who had ruined his lucrative reign in Triblet. At the same moment Magus realized that he had no hope of escape. So he decided he would take at least the chief cause, of his misfortunes with him. Swinging around, he faced Dusty and sent his right hand flying across to the butt of the left side gun.

Dusty cut loose from the bay's back as soon as he saw Magus look in his direction. Swinging his right leg up and over the horse's neck, he thrust himself clear without slackening its speed. Down he plunged, landing running. Once again he fooled his enemy, for Magus never expected him to make such a move. Although the marshal's Colt came out, he had to swing it towards where Dusty came to a halt. Across flashed Dusty's right hand. Half a second later the Peacemaker was in it, lined at Magus and with its hammer starting to fall. Two shots sounded almost as one.

Dusty's hat jerked from his head as if tugged by an invisible hand. At the same moment Kurt Magus pitched over backwards, a hole in the centre of his forehead.

Silence fell after the gun-roaring minutes just ended. Dusty stood in the alley and dropped his Colt into leather. Hearing feet behind him, he turned to look at Mansfield who was approaching on the run.

"It's over, General," Dusty said.

Then people were converging on the alley, citizens of Triblet wanting to learn what was happening in their town, or members of the floating outfit wishing to make sure their leader had suffered no harm.

"I'm Governor Mansfield," Mansfield announced, facing the people and removing his hat.

"By cracky, it's him for sure!" a man confirmed in a loud voice. "I mind him from the War. What's been happening, Governor?"

"I came here to see for myself what a trail end town treated cowhands like," Mansfield replied, cold eyes raking the crowd and causing more than one member of it to move in a restless, guilt-filled manner. "And I've seen it."

"Say," Dusty growled, eyeing Mark, the Kid and Waco coldly. "Just how did you bunch get here so fast?"

They were standing in the bar of the Lone Wolf, while General Mansfield told the citizens of Triblet what he thought of the way their town was run and Doc Leroy attended to the wounded, including the badly beaten outlaw found in the jail. The other three members of the floating outfit had been hoping Dusty would forget the circumstances behind their timely arrival and exchanged glances as if searching for inspiration.

"Waal, it was this ways—" said the Kid. "You tell him, Mark. Us poor unfortunate Injuns ain't learned to lie like you white folks."

"I've just remembered," the blond giant answered, throwing a barbed glare which bounced off the Kid's hide. "There's this right pretty lil gal keeping a cup of coffee waiting for me."

"It'll keep," Dusty informed him.

"It'll go cold," Mark protested.

"All you have to do is tell me how you got here so fast," Dusty insisted.

"Well, it was this way," Mark started. "We—"

"When the wind changed, we figured we'd best move in closer," Waco declared, with the air of a scientist shouting "Eureka" at making an important discovery. "You reckon that lil gal'd run to two cups of coffee, Mark?"

"Could be she'll raise three cups," the Kid drawled and beamed at Dusty. "See, Cap'n Fog, sir, when the wind changed that's just what we figured."

With that the trio turned to leave, their expressions of justification plain for all to see.

"Hold it a dog-goned minute!" Dusty barked. "You figured you ought to move in *when* the wind changed?"

"That's just what we figured," Waco agreed, looking piously into the air.

"Only the wind hadn't changed when we went into the marshal's office," Dusty pointed out.

"He don't believe us!" the Kid told the other two in a shocked voice. "And he didn't go into the marshal's office, he was took there."

"Which same none of us three, 'cept maybe Lon when younger's ever been took to the pokey for evil-doings," Waco went on.

Knowing that he would never be given

confirmation of his suspicions that the others had concocted their own plan, Dusty surrendered.

"All right, all right," he sighed. "I'll say no more about it."

"So you shouldn't for shame," the Kid told him. "As if anybody'd not trust lovable, truthful lil us."

"Go drink your coffee," Dusty ordered. "Likely you've earned it for thinking so fast when the wind changed!"

On returning to the hunting camp with the Texans, Mansfield prepared to hold a long discussion on what he had witnessed in Triblet and use the findings as a basis for better understanding. However the chance did not arise. The same evening they returned, a tall, gangling, mournful-looking cowhand arrived.

"This's Billy Jack, General," Dusty introduced. "He rides for the OD Connected. I told him where we'd be."

"What's up, Billy Jack?" Mark inquired.

"Got word there's been bad trouble up to Trail End," the cowhand, who had been Dusty's sergeant major in the War, replied.

"Figured you'd want to know, Cap'n. Young Lige Dopler was killed there."

"How?" Dusty demanded.

"Him and some of his pards got into a fuss over a faro game at Bellamy's place," Billy Jack answered. "Allowed they was cheated. Which same's likely going by the second-dealer boxes I saw when I went there. Jackley hauled Lige off to jail with the others, only Lige fought back. Rest of 'em was fined and turned loose. They went back to their camp. Next morning when they called for Lige, Jackley told 'em he'd died in the night."

"How'd he die?" Mark growled.

"Town doctor allowed a heart seizure. Only that didn't explain the bruising and stove-in ribs they found when they come to bury Lige. I talked the boys out of going into town with guns, but they're headed down trail to tell Shanghai about it."

Before his visit to Triblet, Mansfield might have thought of the incident as another example of Texans causing trouble. He no longer felt the same way and wondered just how much justification lay behind the accusations of cheating. If the saloon used dealing boxes which allowed the operator to decide to produce the second from the top card if the top one was detrimental to the house, then the cowhands were correct in their assumption. Thinking of the brutally beaten man in the Triblet cells, Mansfield also wondered if the same thing happened in Trail End but with more serious results.

"You've got trouble, General," Dusty said soberly. "Lige Dopler was Shanghai Pierce's favourite nephew. When Shanghai comes up here, he'll be gunning for Jackley and he's a man who can back his play."

"So I've heard," Mansfield replied, recalling the stories which came his way about the tough, efficient Texas fighting rancher, Shanghai Pierce.

"It won't just be a hoorawing either," Dusty warned. "General, this time you could have a shooting war on your hands."

"What would you do?" Mansfield asked, aware that Dusty was speaking the truth and knowing what the result could easily develop into.

"I'd use my powers as Governor to take Jackley out of office and send in a man to investigate Lige's death," Dusty replied. "Shanghai's not unreasonable and's smart enough to see what a shooting fuss might start. If he sees you're trying to straighten things out, he'll hold off and let you do it."

Sitting back in his chair, Mansfield turned over Dusty's suggestions in his mind. As Governor he could remove Jackley from office and appoint a new marshal. The problem being to select a man whom Shanghai Pierce and other Texans would trust. That let out Wyatt Earp and Wild Bill Hickok. Bat Masterson was needed as a restraining influence on the Earp brothers in Dodge City. Nor could Mansfield think of any other Kansas peace officer who might fill the bill.

Then Mansfield realized that the answer sat facing him across the table, probably the one man who could convince Pierce of the Governor's sincerity and desire for better relations with the Texans.

"All right, I'll turn Jackley out," Mansfield said. "Will you go in as marshal for me, Captain Fog?"

Dusty read a challenge in the words. By offering to make a Texan marshal of Trail End, Mansfield had laid his political future on the line. Clearly Mansfield wanted to know if Dusty was also prepared to make a sacrifice in the interests of peace between

Texas and Kansas. There could only be one reply.

"As soon as you can fix for me to start, General," Dusty said.

Part Two

A WIFE FOR DUSTY FOG

IT could not be claimed that Dusty Fog felt
happy or pleased when Miss Martha Jane
Canary walked into the town marshal's
office at Trail End. Yet a casual, unknowing
observer might have wondered why not.
Despite the imposing ring of her name, Miss
Canary looked neither overbearing nor
domineering. In fact one would assume that
her appearance, unconventional though it
might be, ought to make her arrival attractive
to the eyes of a red-blooded young man.

A battered U.S. cavalry kepi perched at a
jaunty angle on a mop of shortish, curly red
hair. While not ravishingly beautiful, her
freckled, good-looking face had a warm,
healthy charm. Under a loose-fitting fringed
buckskin jacket, she wore an open-necked
tartan shirt unbuttoned a mite lower than
might have been regarded as decorous in view
of the garment's snug quality. Like the shirt,
her levis pants appeared to have been bought

a size too small, and shrunk further in washing. She trimmed down from a rich, full bosom to a slender waist without artificial aids, or the tight material of the shirt lied, then curved out to firm hips and shapely legs which ended in low-heeled boots. A long-lashed bull whip coiled from a loop on her waist band, while a gunbelt slanted down her right hip with an ivory-handled Navy Colt, rechambered to take metal cartridges, butt forward in its tied-down, contoured holster.

Miss Canary's choice of attire did not cause Dusty's slight frown as he laid down the pen with which he had been filling in the office's desk log. From various sources, Mark Counter in particular, Dusty knew Miss Canary to be a happy-go-lucky, fun-loving girl whose good qualities included loyalty to her friends, courage and some unorthodox ability. He was also aware that she possessed a penchant for finding and involving her friends in trouble to such an extent that she had earned the name Calamity Jane.

That Calamity should be in Trail End did not surprise Dusty. The girl worked as a driver for a freight outfit and could have come for any number of reasons to do with her employment.

After nodding to the girl, Dusty turned his attention to the couple following somewhat hesitantly on her heels. The man was tall, thin, stoop-shouldered, grey haired, clad in bib-overalls and heavy, low-heeled boots. No younger, the woman had a plump figure and a face that might have carried a happy expression if it were not for the worry lines on it. A sun bonnet hid her hair and she wore an old gingham dress. From their appearance, they were dirt-farmers, poor, struggling to exist in a hard, unpromising land. From the care-worn expressions on their faces, the couple came loaded down with bad trouble.

"Come on in, Tom, Becky," Calamity said cheerfully over her shoulder, then grinned at the small Texan as he rose to greet them. "Howdy, Cap'n Dusty, I fetched these folks in to see you. They need help."

Looking at Dusty, an obvious Texas cowhand despite his wearing the badge of a Kansas town's marshal, the farmer's face showed that he doubted if any help would be forthcoming.

"I don't rightly know if I should bother the marshal—" the man began.

"This here's Tom and Becky Wilson from out on the Deccan Valley, Cap'n Dusty,"

Calamity interrupted, ignoring the old farmer's hesitation. "They run a small place up there. Leastwise, they did until some stinking, fancy-talking sidewinder slickered 'em out of it. I met 'em on the trail and when they told me what'd happened, I had 'em come with me so's you could get their place back for them."

"What happened, friend?" Dusty asked, deciding that his fears about Miss Canary's arrival heralding trouble had been justifiable.

"Now you tell everything that happened, Tom Wilson," Calamity ordered, glancing to where Waco was entering the office from the cell area at the rear of the building, and then continuing with the matter in hand. "Soon's Cap'n Dusty hears, he'll fix your sorrows easier'n falling off a log."

With that she perched her rump on the corner of Dusty's desk and sat swinging a shapely, muscular leg. Her whole attitude implied that she had done everything necessary for the solution of the couple's problems and she could now relax.

For a moment the farmer stood silent, exchanging glances with his wife. Little in their previous experience with Texas cowhands led them to believe they might expect assistance from one of that wild, reckless, fun-seeking breed. Then the woman looked at Dusty, sensing his personal magnetism, strength and a sympathy with them in their time of stress. She felt that if any man could help them, it was the *big* Texan behind the desk. So she nodded approval to her husband's unasked question.

"It's this ways, Cap'n," Wilson said, shuffling forward and removing his hat. "We've got this little place up in the Deccan Valley. Twarn't nothing much, but it done for me 'n' the missus. Then these six fellers come to see us. One of 'em was a for-real, high-toned, big-city gent called Stubel. He shows me a paper that allows he's from the Government and sent out to take over our land to build a fort for the Army—"

"Lying son-of-a-bitch," Calamity interjected *sotto voce*.

"Did you read the paper he showed you?" Dusty inquired.

"Su—" the man began.

"Tom don't read, marshal," the woman put in. "There's no shame to it."

"No, ma'am," Dusty agreed. "No shame at

all. I suppose this Stubel read it for you, Mr. Wilson?"

"He did," Wilson replied. "Then allows that the Government's taking my land and I've got to sell to him, like it or not. Says they have to put the fort there because the surveys shows it's the best military place."

"Have you seen any survey?" Waco asked, joining Dusty behind the desk.

"Couple of fellers come through maybe three months back making one," Wilson answered.

"Soldiers?" Dusty asked.

"They didn't wear uniforms."

"I never saw Army surveyors who didn't," Calamity commented.

"Well, Cap'n," Wilson continued. "Mr. Stubel pays me two hundred dollars on account and says I'll get the rest when I hand in a paper to the Mulrooney land office. Allowed me 'n' Becky should go straight there so's we can apply for a new piece of land that's waiting for us."

"The Government can't just turn honest folk off their land that ways, can they Cap'n Dusty?" Calamity asked.

"I reckon they could, but this whole business doesn't sit right," Dusty replied.

"Did you sign anything, Mr. Wilson?"

"Put my mark on three papers after Mr. Stubel read 'em to me."

"He read all three?"

"Only the top one. Allowed the other two was just copies. Which figured seeing's how he works for the Government."

"Do you have one of the papers with you?"

"Nope," Wilson admitted. "He allowed that the land office in Mulrooney knew all about me. All I had to do was hand in the paper he wrote out and signed."

"Can I see it?" Dusty asked.

Reaching into his back pocket, Wilson extracted a thin wallet and removed a folded sheet of paper from it.

"This's i—" he began, opening out the paper. Then he stopped speaking and stared down. "Wha—?"

Dusty took the paper, while Calamity and Waco leaned over to look at it.

"There's nothing on it!" the girl gasped. "Are you sure this's the right one, Tom?"

"Sure I'm sure. I put it right into my wallet when I got it."

"Where'd he get the pen and ink to write it?" Dusty went on, holding the paper up so that he could look with a light behind it.

"From his bag, the pen," Wilson replied. "Carried his ink in one of them fancy vest pocket pots."

"Disappearing ink, Dusty?" Waco guessed.

"Looks that way," the small Texan agreed. "There's some you can bring back one way or another, others that look good until they dry out, then fade off all the way. I'd bet this was written with the sort you can't bring back."

"They've been slickered!" Calamity stated emphatically. "I knowed it as soon as they said the feller sent them to Mulrooney instead of coming here which's closer to their place."

"I'd've figured you to go busting after them yahoos head down, horns hooking and dainty lil feet a-pawing the dirt, Calam," Waco grinned.

"Likely I would have if I hadn't remembered who's running the law here," the girl replied. "Knowed there wasn't no need for it then. If you want an extra deputy to ride in the posse, Cap'n Dusty, I'm free to come along."

Sitting down behind the desk, Dusty let out a long sigh. The moment he had dreaded since Calamity made her appearance was at hand. While he knew that the girl had come in good faith and because of her respect and high regard for him, she had placed too much reliance on his being able to help.

"You know that I can't take a posse out after them, Calam," Dusty said quietly and waited for the explosion, which did not take long to come.

Bouncing off the desk, Calamity leaned across it and stared into Dusty's face. "Why not?" she yelped. "Tom and Becky's been slickered—"

"Likely, but there's no proof they have yet," Dusty replied. "I'm not saying they're lying, afore you swell up and bust. What you're forgetting is I'm only marshal of Trail End, Calam. My jurisdiction ends with the city limits."

"Hell fire!" Calamity blazed, ignoring what she knew to be the truth. "Tom and Becky worked right hard on their place. Now they've been slickered out of it and you tell me the law can't help them?"

"I'm saying that I can't help them, Calam," Dusty corrected.

"I never thought I'd see the day when Dusty Fog'd turn his back on folks in trouble!" the girl snorted.

"Damn it, Calam!" Waco growled, filled with indignation at the unwarranted attack on his idol. "If you'd use any brains you've got in that hot head, you'd know Dusty's hands're tied."

"Don't you talk to me like that, you lippy button!" she screeched back. "I'll—Oh to hell with it! Come on, Tom. Let's do what you said, go see that fancy talking law wrangler."

"Look, Mr. Wilson," Dusty said gently. "I'm sorry that I can't just ride out and take your place back, but I've no legal standing outside Trail End. I'll telegraph the county sheriff—"

"And he'll likely be too busy getting ready for the Fourth of July parade to help!" Calamity snorted. "Come on, Tom. Let's go see that lawyer and if he can't help, I'll round up some fellers who will."

With that she thrust herself from the desk and stamped out of the room. Dusty opened his mouth to give a warning but the man and woman also turned. Disappointment showed on their faces as they followed the girl from the office. Infected by Calamity's enthusiasm, they had come to Trail End expecting a miraculous solution to the difficulties and felt cheated when it failed to materialize.

Letting out a long sigh, Dusty took up his pen but did not start writing in the log. Waco watched his friend's face and guessed how Dusty felt at being forced to refuse the old couple's request for help. Yet the youngster could not see any way in which Dusty might help them.

Undoubtedly the Wilson's had been cheated out of their property; but it took place beyond the city limits, in an area where Dusty had no right to enforce the law. More than that the small Texan faced enough difficulties handling the clean-up of Trail End without outside distractions. Already the Texans had made improvements; the former marshal, Jackley, died trying to murder Dusty after being forcibly ejected from office and two of the worst saloons were closed after being caught out in illegal practices. However Waco knew there was much more to be done before Shanghai Pierce accepted that Trail End was purged and clean.

"Damn that Calamity!" Dusty growled, tossing aside his pen. "Why the hell did she have to bring them here?"

"Same reason as I'd've done it," Waco replied. "Because she figured you're the best man to help them."

130

"Which I can't do," Dusty pointed out bitterly. "And when word gets around that I didn't, folks'll say it's because I don't want to help nesters."

"Anybody who'd believe that'd be hawg-stupid!" Waco snorted.

"There're plenty who'll want to believe, and who'll pretend to even though they know it's a lie," Dusty told him. "It'll be mighty fine fodder to use against General Mansfield and us."

"Would Mayor Galt be one of 'em who wants to believe it?"

"He's just a sticky-fingered small town politician, boy. I'm thinking of the soft-shells and their kind. Something like this'd give them a mighty big edge in stirring up hard feelings against the General."

"Time was when I thought all a lawman did was walk around town and toss drunks in the hoosegow," Waco said. "What're you fixing to do?"

"Take a walk to the telegraph office and send for answers to some questions."

"And then?" Waco inquired.

"Then I'm going to get on with my work," Dusty replied and eyed the youngster coldly. "Don't you have some to do?"

"Sure," Waco replied, unabashed. "Only I hoped I'd talked you into forgetting about it."

Although still muttering her indignation, Calamity had barely left the office before she started to regret her outburst at Dusty. Equally, being Calamity, she would willingly have undergone torture rather than return and admit it. Then something happened to bring her contrition boiling over.

Neither Calamity nor the Wilson's spoke for some time as they walked in the direction of the lawyer's office. Then the old farmer let out a disappointed sigh.

"I never figured a Texan'd help the likes of us," he said.

Instantly Calamity's sense of fair play and loyalty took control of her emotions, although the twinges of her conscience helped direct her actions. She realized how baseless Wilson's charge was and the manner in which it might be interpreted if repeated before a larger audience. Catching the man's arm, she turned him towards her. An indignant face thrust close to Wilson's startled features and a sturdy forefinger prodded him hard in the chest.

"Don't you ever go *thinking* such a fool notion, Tom Wilson!" she hissed. "We both should've knowed a town marshal couldn't touch them jaspers out in the Valley. And I'll bet right now Cap'n Dusty's figuring all which ways how he can help you."

"He sure didn't act like he wanted to do—" Wilson began then he stared by the girl. "Well I'll be—!"

"What's up?" Calamity asked, turning to see what had attracted his attention.

Following the direction of Wilson's gaze, Calamity saw two men strolling along the opposite sidewalk. Both were tall, well-built, dressed in range clothes, yet she knew they could not be called cowhands. The Colts in the tied-down holsters hung significantly to West-wise eyes and their general attitude marked them as professional fighting men.

Instead of answering the girl's question, Wilson set off across the street. Mrs. Wilson supplied Calamity with the necessary information.

"Oh, Lord!" the woman gasped.

"What is it, Becky?" Calamity demanded.

"They were with the bunch that took our place," Mrs. Wilson replied. "Tom must be

133

going to ask them about that disappearing ink."

"The crazy old coot!" Calamity gasped and started across the street, to be halted by a group of cowhands galloping along in search of somewhere to spend their trail's end pay.

"Look who's coming over here, Dirk," the bigger of the men remarked, a grin twisting the lips under a heavy moustache. "It's that fool nester the boss took early yesterday, ain't it?"

"Yeah," the other answered, his lean face showing cold calculation mingled with real cruelty.

"What in hell's he doing? He was supposed to head for Mulrooney."

"Could be he looked at the paper, Jigger," Dirk commented.

"What'll we do?"

"Let him start something if he wants. Then we'll make sure he don't go wailing to the marshal about being rooked."

If either of the men noticed Calamity start to follow Wilson, they attached no importance to her. By the time the wild-riding cowhands had swept past, Wilson had reached the sidewalk and confronted the pair.

134

"All right!" he said in a threatening manner. "What's the game?"

"Means us, I reckon, Jigger," Dirk said. "You know him?"

"Never seed him afore," Jigger replied in a carrying voice. "What's eating at you, pop?"

"You know damned well what's eating me!" Wilson spat back, conscious that a few other users of the sidewalk and a group of loafers seated on a bench outside a barber's shop were watching and listening.

"Reckon he's crazy, Dirk?" Jigger asked. "He acts a mite tetched in the head. Had an uncle got took that way one time. He like to kill a feller he'd never met afore."

All the anger and frustration boiling inside Wilson erupted at the scornful, mocking words. Not content with stealing his home, the two men seemed set on making him look a fool in front of the on-lookers. So he advanced closer than prudence dictated, forgetting that he was no longer the tough young rooster who revelled in fighting.

"Best walk on by him," Dirk suggested in the same aggravating tone.

"Like hell you will!" Wilson shouted and lunged with hands grabbing at Jigger, the nearer of his taunters.

Immediately the man gripped the front of Wilson's bib-overalls and swung him around. Struggling together, although Jigger used less than his full strength, they crossed the sidewalk to collide with the wall of the nearest building. With Wilson backed against the wall and partially hidden from the onlookers, Jigger caught the farmer's left wrist and forced it down in the direction of his Colt's butt.

"Don't you try to pull my gun!" Jigger yelled, wanting to implant the idea of doing so in Wilson's mind and direct the witnesses' attention to it should the old man do so.

Coming up on to the sidewalk, Calamity heard the words and saw the plan with shocking clarity. Already Wilson's fingers were closing awkwardly on the Colt's butt, with Jigger pretending to be trying to stop it leaving the holster. The moment Wilson drew the gun, the second of the hardcases would shoot him down and claim to have acted to save his friend's life.

In her excitement and hurry to prevent Wilson from being killed, Calamity committed an error in tactics.

"Don't do it, Tom!" she yelled, springing

forward with her hand fanning across to the handle of the whip.

Just an instant too late she realized that she ought to have held a weapon before making her presence known. Turning fast, Dirk brought up his left hand to place its palm on her face and shove. Sent backwards and to the side, Calamity hit the hitching rail. Anger at the treatment wiped out discretion, as it often had in Calamity's eventful young life. Bouncing from the rail, she rushed forward.

Once more Dirk showed the speed with which he could move. The left hand stabbed forward again, not in a punch but as a more effective way of dealing with an angry female. Savagely Dirk closed his fingers on the firm mound of Calamity's left breast, sinking the thumb in from the other side to aid the crushing pressure.

Pain bit into the girl, numbing her thoughts so as to prevent her from acting with her usual effective ability. Forgetting the whip and gun at her belt, she grabbed at Dirk's wrist with both hands and tried to pull the cruelly-tightening fingers from her flesh.

"You keep out of things that don't—" Dirk began, fingers working on the trapped breast and unaware of the big, menacing figure approaching rapidly from along the street.

Dirk learned soon enough of Mark Counter's presence. Brought out of the barber's shop, where he had been awaiting a haircut, by the sound of the struggle, the blond giant saw Calamity in trouble and sprang to her assistance. Passing Jigger and Wilson, he reached out with his big right hand towards the unsuspecting Dirk.

Fingers with the power of steel clamps closed on the hardcase's neck from behind, driving pain through him and causing him to release his hold on Calamity. Staggering across to the hitching rail, she clutched at her throbbing bust and stared at the men in front of her.

With a surging heave, Mark swung Dirk to the rear and then propelled him the other way. A good-sized man, Dirk found to his amazement that his unseen assailant handled him as if he weighed no more than a child in arms. Not that he thought for long on the matter. Sent shooting forward by the powerful thrust, he struck the hitching rail alongside Calamity, rolled over it without being able to halt his progress and landed flat on his back at the edge of the street.

Seeing Mark's intervention, Jigger decided to take a hand. He also figured a man that strong should be handled from a distance rather than at close quarters. So he struck down hard, knocking Wilson's hand from the Colt. Thrusting the old man aside, Jigger grabbed at the gun himself.

"Look out feller!" Wilson yelled and lunged back to catch hold of Jigger's wrist.

Whirling around, Mark saw Jigger with the Colt half drawn and Wilson trying to prevent it clearing leather. With a snarl, Jigger kicked sideways. His boot crashed into Wilson's shin and brought a croak of pain. The kick also caused the old man to loose his hold and Jigger tore himself free—but too late.

Already Mark was moving into the attack, right hand smoothly scooping the off-side Colt from its holster. If Jigger had completed his draw, Mark would have shot him. However Wilson's intervention prevented the need for that. Around swung Mark's right arm, laying the barrel of the Colt alongside Jigger's jaw. During his time as a deputy in Quiet Town and Mulrooney, Mark had learned to gauge how much power he put behind such a blow. With his strength he might easily have broken the man's jaw, or worse, but he held back on the power. For all that Jigger went down like a pole-axed steer, sprawling unmoving on the sidewalk.

Sitting up, Dirk spat out a curse and his eyes focused on Mark's back. The hard-case realized that only the blond giant among the on-lookers possessed sufficient strength to handle him in such a manner and prepared to take revenge. Sliding the revolver from his holster, he began to lift it to point at the big Texan's back.

Although watching how Mark dealt with Jigger, Calamity did not forget her attacker. Hearing his voice spitting out an obscene word, she turned. One glance told her all she needed to know. Unless something was done fast, Mark stood a chance of taking a bullet in the back. Calamity figured that she was in the best position to help out.

Swiftly she brought up her hands to catch hold of the bottom of the rail. With a heave, she swung herself beneath it and landed alongside Dirk. Giving his full attention to the men on the sidewalk, he failed to see the new danger. After felling Jigger, the big blond turned with a speed that warned Dirk what kind of man he faced. Even without that peace officer's badge on his shirt, the giant

Texan would be a deadly danger and no man to be treated lightly. So Dirk concentrated on Mark and failed to give Calamity's actions any notice until too late.

Before the hard-case could realize the danger, Calamity launched up her left leg in a kick. Ever since the time she fought a *Creole* girl well-versed in the art of *savate*, Calamity had formed a high opinion of the feet as weapons. She had no cause for complaint as the boot drove up under Dirk's hand and sent the gun flying from it.

Snarling his fury, Dirk started to turn on his new attacker. Whatever faults of reck-lessness Calamity might occasionally show, she always tried to avoid making the same mistake twice. Having already received painful proof of how fast the man could move, she knew better than to take unneces-sary chances. Even as she kicked, her right hand slid the whip from its belt loop. Up that close she could not make use of its long lash, but came out just fine despite of that. Swinging up, the weighted handle made a whistling arc and descended with some force on Dirk's head. Having lost his hat while going over the rail, Dirk's skull lacked even that protection against the attack. His fingers were closing on Calamity's leg, so fast did he react, when the whip's handle landed. Immediately the grip relaxed, the hand fell away and he flopped limply on to his back.

That ought to have ended the attack, but Calamity's bust still throbbed its painful reminder of Dirk's treatment. While a good-hearted girl, Calamity did not lightly forgive sins against her. At least, not until she had handed out a few in return. With that in mind, she turned towards the man. Dropping to ram a knee into his chest, she swung the whip up for another blow.

"Calam!" Mark yelled, leaping towards her. "Quit that!"

For a moment the whip, capable of splitting the man's skull if used with all her strength, quivered in the air. Then slowly Calamity lowered her arm and stood up to face the big Texan.

"Can't I whomp him just an itsy-bitsy one?" she asked.

"You was like to bust his head," Mark growled. "Just what in hell've you stirred up this time, Calamity?"

"So help me, Mark," the girl protested. "I never started anything—this time."

Hobbling to the edge of the sidewalk and

holding off his wife who had crossed the street, Wilson spoke in Calamity's defence.

"They're two of a bunch that cheated me out of my farm, mister."

"Did, huh?" Mark said. "Then jail's the place for them, don't you reckon so, Dusty?"

The latter part came as the small Texan arrived. On his way to send telegraph messages requesting information on the Wilson business, Dusty had seen the trouble and headed for it. By the time he arrived, he found that Mark had the situation in hand and heard Wilson's words. An idea began to form in Dusty's fertile brain. One which, if it worked, might solve the old nester's problems.

"I reckon it is," Dusty agreed. "Get some of these fellers to help tote them down there. Calam, go to Bella Union and tell Doc Leroy I want him *pronto*."

"It's done," the girl replied and departed immediately.

"You reckon they're hurt bad enough to need Doc?" Mark inquired.

"It never pays to take chances," Dusty replied. "You go get a room at the hotel, Mr. Wilson. I'll send for you when they start taking notice again and you can swear out your complaint against them."

143

Sitting on a bunk in one of the jail's cells, Dirk touched the top of his head and groaned. On the opposite bunk, Jigger lay holding his swollen jaw. Dirk looked around him, through the bars separating him from the next cell in which a small Texas cowhand lay apparently sleeping off a session of drinking. Then Dirk lifted his eyes to the window and scowled as he saw the position of the sun. From all appearances almost two hours had passed since the girl clubbed him down with her whip.

Although Dirk had been conscious for some minutes, he waited to allow an improvement in his condition before making any move. At last he felt that he could think well enough to talk with the peace officers who had brought him to jail. Rising, he lurched across to the door.

"Hey!" he yelled, hanging on to the bars. "Where's somebody?"

"Want something?" asked the Ysabel Kid, coming through the connecting door to the office.

"Yeah. What am I doing here?"

"Making one helluva noise. You'll wake up the other guests happen you keep at it."

"Damn it!" Dirk snorted. "I mean why've you got us in here?"

"For jumping and whomping a feller 'n' gal in the street, the marshal told me," answered the Kid.

"That old goat started it!" Jigger growled, joining Dirk at the door.

"Sure hope the judge reckons so," the Kid replied.

"I want to see Lawyer Grosvenor," Dirk stated, trying to sound polite.

"What's up in there, Lon?" called a voice from the office.

"One of them jaspers you hauled in wants to see the law wrangler."

"Is that the marshal?" Dirk asked.

"You might say that," drawled the Kid.

"Lemme talk to him."

"Feller wants to talk to you," announced the Kid.

"Fetch him in here," ordered the voice from beyond the connecting door.

Unlocking the cell's door, the Kid stood aside and allowed Dirk to walk by him. However he refused to let Jigger out, declaring that the marshal said he wanted to see "him", not "them". Turning, Dirk told Jigger to sit and wait. Despite the Kid's concern, the noise did not appear to have disturbed the jail's other "guest" for he still lay facing the wall and snoring gently.

On entering the office, Dirk scowled at the sight of the man behind the desk. It was the blond giant who had handled him with such apparent ease on the street. Then Dirk remembered who ran the law in Trail End. It seemed that all the stories about Dusty Fog's exceptional size and strength had a considerable basis of truth. One thing Dirk knew for certain; he must shelve his antagonism and play careful if he hoped to get out of the difficulty in which he found himself.

"What've you got me and my pard locked up for, marshal?" Dirk asked, eyeing the badge on the other's shirt for a moment.

"Assault," Mark Counter replied, satisfied that the man did not suspect the deception being played on him. "I figured you to be a couple of drunks when I saw you rough-handling that old nester and the gal. So I cut in and quietened you."

"That crazy old cuss jumped us," Dirk protested, speaking slowly as he put his thoughts to words. "Allowed we'd slickered him out of his farm."

"That's what he told us," Mark answered.

"Have you slickered him out of it?" drawled Waco, leaning against the weapon rack on the wall.

"The hell we have! Our boss bought the place legal, paid good money for it," Dirk replied, pausing before going on as if a thought just struck him. "Say. Maybe he's trying to get his farm back now he's got the money for it, and jumped us knowing you'd be on hand to look out for him, so's folk'd think he told the truth."

"Is that what you reckon?" inquired the Kid.

"Hell, Cap'n Fog here saw it. That old cuss went for us and tried to grab my pard's gun. Only a crazy man, or somebody wanting folks to think he was crazy'd try a game like that."

"You mean he wanted us to think he'd been driven to desperation by you cheating him out of his farm," Mark suggested. "Figuring maybe I'd shoot one or both of you afore you could explain?"

"It could be," Dirk agreed, delighted by the way "Dusty Fog" appeared to be accepting his story. "Some of them old nesters're smart'n a fox."

"How about the girl you laid hands on."

For a moment Dirk did not reply to Mark's

147

question. Of all the affair, that aspect would take the most answering away. Then Dirk felt a flash of inspiration and proceeded to put it to the test.

"When she come running up, I figured she'd best be out of the way in case lead started flying," he told the listening Texans. "So I shoved her back. Only she come at me again, looking wilder'n a gut-shot bobcat. So I just grabbed out to hold her off."

"That's what happened?" Mark drawled.

"That's just how it happened," Dirk agreed and tried to put an expression of ingratiating magnanimity on his face. "I don't blame you for jumping me, Cap'n Fog. You couldn't know the play and I can guess how it must've looked to you."

"And you reckon you bought this place legal and proper?"

"The feller we work for did. He sent me into Trail End with the bill-of-sale so's the Land Office can transfer the title to our company."

"Go down and take a look, Waco," Mark ordered.

"Yo!" the youngster replied.

"How about me?" Dirk demanded as the youngster left the room.

"I'm holding you until we've squared the rights of this business."

"Then I want to see Lawyer Grosvenor."

"Go ask him to come along after you've seen this feller back into his cell, Lon," Mark said. "And while you're out, see if you can find the other two. They ought to be back from their rounds by now."

A slight frown creased Dirk's forehead as he returned uncomplainingly to the cells. There had been three of the floating outfit in the office, leaving two unaccounted for. While "Dusty Fog" had made it appear they were out walking the rounds, that could be to lull the prisoner's suspicions. Maybe one or both of them were waiting outside the cell hoping to hear some scrap of incriminating conversation.

Or maybe—Dirk looked to where the small cowhand lay on the bunk, still apparently asleep. Could he be one of the missing deputies? Dirk threw off the idea as preposterous. By all accounts Mark Counter ran Dusty Fog a close second in size and heft, while Doc Leroy was a tall, lean cuss. That short runt, in his trail dirty clothes, could not be a member of the floating outfit. Most likely he was a wrangler or cook's louse for the trail crew which arrived just before the fight; an insignificant nobody who had been brought to jail for his own protection after falling into a drunken stupor.

For all that, Dirk felt uneasy. His every instinct told him that something was wrong. What, he could not decide but he trusted those warning instincts. So he shook his head in silent, grim command as Jigger seemed about to ask a question. Not until the Kid had left the passage and closed the door behind him did Dirk offer to let Jigger speak.

"What happened?"

"I told them our story," Dirk replied. "How the boss bought that place legal and we come to town to fix up the sale with the Land Office. I reckon that old cuss's trying to get it back."

Directing another warning glare at Jigger, Dirk went on to tell him the story fabricated in the office. At no time did Dirk give a hint that he had made up the excuse on the spur of the moment.

"Reckon they believed you?" Jigger finally asked.

"They're going to check with the Land Office," Dirk answered. "And they'll find he sold us the place, put his mark to the bill-of-sale."

"I never figured we'd run into trouble here," Jigger complained. "The boss reckoned Trail End was the best town for us."

"Only he didn't know Dusty Fog's been put in as marshal," Dirk pointed out.

"And he's safe on the Deccan, headed for the State line—" Jigger began.

Striding forward, Dirk faced the other man and, big though he was, Jigger shrank back before his fury.

"Shut your mouth and keep it shut!" Dirk snarled. "Once the lawyer gets here we'll get everything fixed. Until then, if you want to keep your teeth, keep your fool lips closed over 'em."

"Sure, Dirk," Jigger muttered. "I only thought—"

"Well don't! Or talk. If they have you in the office and ask questions, say just what I told you, nothing more. Or better still, don't say anything until you've got Grosvenor at your side."

Listening to the words as he lay on the bunk in the next cell, Dusty Fog recognized that his gamble had failed to produce a win.

151

When he first learned the identity of the two men, Dusty saw what he hoped would be a chance to obtain proof of the land swindle. So he had them carried to the jail and placed in a cell. Fetched by Calamity, Doc Leroy made sure that the men did not recover prematurely by administering judicious doses of chloroform from the small medical kit he carried in his warbag. So effectively did Doc perform his work, that Dusty found time to make all the necessary arrangements before the pair recovered.

Searching Dirk and Jigger produced nothing to connect them with the land swindle. However a telegraph message to the nearest army post brought the prompt, if expected, answer that no fort was planned in the Deccan Valley. Wanting concrete evidence on which to act, Dusty changed into a set of dirtied-up old work clothes and, before the men came back to consciousness, entered the next cell. He hoped that his pose as a cowhand sleeping off a drunk might be successful. It had. Clearly Dirk accepted Mark as Dusty, but he still refused to say anything incriminating.

From past experience Dusty knew how to act next; he had seen enough young cowhands wake up in similiar circumstances to be convincing. Certainly the men in the next cell showed no suspicion as, after grunting, groaning and tossing around on the bunk, Dusty sat up.

"Lord lord, never again!" Dusty groaned, keeping his face partially concealed by his hands. Then he lurched to his feet and crossed to the door, raising his voice in a feeble yell. "Hey!"

Coming into the passage before the cells, the Kid grinned at Dusty. "See you woke up, Billy boy."

"How'd I get here?" Dusty asked.

"Come in sleeping like a babe. Marshal figured you'd be best off in here for a spell. What'd you been drinking?"

"Dunno. But I'll never touch another drop's long's I live."

"Want to bet?" the Kid said, having crossed the passage and unlocked the door during the preceding conversation.

"Hey!" Dirk growled. "You was supposed to be going for our lawyer."

"And I'll do it," the Kid answered. "Was just going when Billy here yelled. So I come in. When he wakes up, he has to go *pronto*, or we get a wet cell."

Taking the hint, Dusty left the cell and

went into the office like a man who found urgent need to relieve the pangs of nature. The Kid followed, promising to start out after the law wrangler right off, and closed the connecting door.

"Anything?" Mark inquired.

"Not much," Dusty answered, joining the big blond at the desk. "That jasper you had in's too smart to talk. All I know is the rest of the bunch's still out and buying land."

"Let's go after 'em and haul 'em back here," suggested the Kid.

"Even if the sherrif'd make us temporary deputies, which's not likely from the way he answered when I asked him coming down here, we'd still have to find them."

"They're on the Deccan," Mark pointed out.

"They were on the Deccan last we heard," Dusty corrected. "Only one of those jaspers in the cell allows the rest of the bunch're headed north for the State Line. Which means we'd have to start hunting for them."

"You figure I couldn't trail five of 'em?" drawled the Kid.

"Sure you could," Dusty replied. "But leave us not forget we've got this town to hold down."

"Three of us could handle it, even two of us, for a spell," Mark said.

"Like you say, Mark, for a spell. Only we don't know how long it'd take us to catch up to that bunch, even if we had anything on them so's we could bring them in!"

Before any more could be said, Waco entered the office carrying a roll of stiff white paper in one hand.

"You got 'em, Dusty?" he inquired in a tone which implied the answer would be in the affirmative.

"Not so's you'd notice," Dusty answered. "What's that?"

"Bill-of-sale for the Wilson place and a map," the youngster replied, sweeping Mark's expensive Stetson from the desk top so that he could spread open his trophy.

"Hey, that's my hat!" Mark growled.

"*Bueno*," grinned the youngster. "I thought it was a good one."

"One of these days—!" Mark growled, retrieving his property.

"Land-sakes, making all that fuss over a cheap ole woosey," Waco replied, ready to take hurried evasive action.

However Mark refused to be goaded. Instead he dusted his hat with extravagant

155

care and said, "Go on, tell us all this important news you're getting puffed up and sassy over."

"Seems like the Army's going to build a whole string of forts along the Deccan," Waco announced. "Those fellers brought in six bills-of-sale. I've got the places they bought marked on the map."

Removing the sheet of paper which had been rolled inside the map, Dusty looked down. Slowly he ran his forefinger from one of Waco's marks to the next, then continued the line.

"They're working their way north-west," he said quietly, yet his three companions tensed and exchanged glances. "Happen they keep on that line, they'll soon be level with Trail End. Trouble being that they've not bought every place they came to."

"Could be some of the owners wouldn't sell," Mark suggested.

"Or maybe they didn't get asked 'cause they could read and write," Waco went on.

"How's that, boy?" Dusty demanded.

"None of them fellers who sold out could write," the youngster elaborated. "'Leastways, they all signed their bill-of-sale with a cross, not a name."

"How in hell would they know who can read and who can't?" asked the Kid.

"Check on the land office records, maybe," Dusty replied. "Go get Mr. Wilson and Calamity, Lon."

"If I'd've kept quiet, likely you'd've forgot I was here," grumbled the Kid as he walked across the office. "You white folks's allus picking on us poor, uneducated Injuns."

"Damned if he won't want us to sell him Manhattan Island back for what they paid for it next," Mark sniffed and eyed Waco up then down. "Still, when you look at some folks, Injuns aren't so bad."

Carrying out Dusty's order proved remarkably simple. On leaving the office, the Kid found the people he sought approaching. So he waited on the sidewalk before the door until they arrived, delivered the message and ushered them into Dusty's presence with the smug air of one who had just completed a difficult task.

"You sent for us, Cap'n Dusty?" Calamity asked, eyes aglow with eagerness.

"Why in hell do you reckon I *walked* all that way to find you?" the Kid growled and hopped hurriedly aside as her foot lashed at

157

his shin. "Damned if I hadn't ought to've let that buzz saw get you."

"Why in hell didn't you then?" the girl challenged, recalling with a barely concealed shudder how the Kid had saved her from an extremely unpleasant death when a vicious, power-mad woman tied her on a log which was started moving towards a circular saw.

"I thought on it when I saw you there," grinned the Kid. "Then I figured that one of you's more'n enough to have around. Two'd like to drive everybody *loco*."

"Why don't you pair go play mumbly-peg in the corral?" Dusty barked.

"He cheats," replied the unabashed Calamity.

"She won't let me win," explained the Kid in the same breath.

Coming around the table, Mark took hold of the Kid's shoulder with his left hand and hooked the right through Calamity's waistband. Directing the Kid, who knew better than to resist, and carrying Calamity as she almost turned the air blue with curses, Mark dumped them in the corner of the room.

"Now maybe we can get some work done," Dusty said and held out the second item brought by Waco from the Land Office. "Did you sign this, Mr. Wilson?"

"It sure looks like my mark," the old man replied after studying the document. "I don't recollect what it be though."

"It's a bill-of-sale for your farm," Dusty explained, "and says that you sold out to the Mid-Western Land Syndicate for two thousand, two hundred dollars."

"I never signed no such—!"

"Hold your voice down, friend," Dusty ordered, yet his tone was gentle. "I don't want those pair in the cells to hear. You're sure this's your mark?"

"Sure, but I never—"

"They didn't offer you that much for your place?"

"That's just what they offered me. Only I was to get the two thousand from the Land Office in Mulrooney."

"Only this claims you've received full payment already," Dusty pointed out. "In other words, you're not entitled to one red cent more from them."

"That does it. That does *it*!" Calamity yelped, bounding from the corner and glaring at Dusty across the desk. "Now either you

159

take out after that bunch, or so help me, I will."

"Choke off, if you want to help this gent like you claim!" Dusty growled and the girl fell silent. "Did you go see Lawyer Grosvenor, Mr. Wilson?"

"Sure," the old man admitted. "Only I never mentioned them two in the cells."

"What'd he say?"

"Took a twenty dollar retainer off me and promised he'd start working on it right, straight off."

"Can he do anything?" Calamity asked bluntly.

"Not much, I'd say," Dusty replied. "Seeing's how he's working for the other side as well."

"Why that cheap, side-winding son-of-a-bitch—!" Calamity flared up. "He can't pull a game like that can he?"

"This bill-of-sale, Mr. Wilson," Dusty said, ignoring the question. "It's got your mark, witnessed by a 'T. A. Salt'."

"I don't know any—" Wilson began. "Hey though! The others called the feller who witnessed me make my mark on them papers 'Salty'." Then his face became troubled as he realized what his remembrance meant. "But they told me they was working for the Government and that I had to sell. All Mr. Stubel give me was two hundred dollars."

"Tom wouldn't lie, Cap'n Dusty," Calamity stated.

"I don't reckon he is lying," Dusty assured her. "Trouble being these fellers have what looks like a legal bill-of-sale and he's got nothing to show it isn't."

"They told him a stinking pack of lies to make him sell!" Calamity protested.

"And they're going to stand up afore a judge, all honest and truthful, and tell him they done womped up a stinking pack of lies to cheat this gent out of his land?" Waco asked, ready to take cover if the girl turned her frustrated fury on him.

However Calamity remained calm, ominously so in Mark's experienced opinion.

"I reckon we could maybe make them feel like doing it," she cooed, gently stroking the handle of her whip.

"Real easy," seconded the Kid in a mild, almost angelic voice which would have sent many men along the Rio Grande's bloody banks hunting for cover.

"Why don't you pair get hitched?" Mark growled. "You'd raise a brood of bloodthirsty buttons all eager to start wrapping their school-ma'am in a green hide, or staking her out on an ant-hill.''

"Don't know as how I should go around with such evil-thinking folks," Waco continued. "Me being so young, sweet, innocent and lovable and all.''

"What Mark and Waco're trying to say, *Miss Canary*," Dusty finished dryly. "And which *Lon* ought to know without telling, is that taking those fellers into court all bruised and cut up won't get Tom here his place back. Knowing he's been slickered's one thing. Proving it legally's a horse of a different colour. Grosvenor's a slick law wrangler and they can likely hire better if they need to.''

"So what do you figure to do?" Calamity demanded.

"Best way to nail their hides to the wall'd be catch 'em at their game," Mark suggested.

"So you figure to sit around on your butt-ends and wait for 'em to come and try to slicker you out of the jail-house?''

"That'd give us just what we want, Calam," Dusty admitted. "Only I can't see them being obliging enough to do it.''

162

"Nor me, comes to that!" Calamity replied, bristling sarcasm.

"Comes to a real smart point," Dusty went on, dropping a finger to the map and running it from Trail End to a point on the Deccan River. "There's only one way I can see us getting Tom's place back."

"How?" Calamity asked.

"By catching them, like Mark said."

"You'd have to be there when they did it to catch 'em that ways."

"I figure to be," Dusty answered.

"And they'll try to pull a land-steal in front of Dusty Fog?" Calamity sniffed. "I believe in fairies, but—"

"They'll be trying it in front of a young nester who can't read nor write," Dusty corrected and eyed the girl speculatively. "And his wife, who's had no more schooling'll be stood watching it."

"With us bunch hid in the root cellar, listening with all our tiny ears?" Calamity enthused. Then her face lost its smile. "How do we find 'em just calling on this here nester?"

"We'll look for him on the Deccan north of here," Dusty replied.

"You'll be taking one helluva chance doing

it, Dusty," Mark warned, guessing what his *amigo* had in mind. "Should anything happen while you're away—"

Mark did not mean just the physical risk involved, although that might prove considerable. To reach the area in which the gang would be operating meant an absence from Trail End of at least three days. During that time any trouble which developed in town would be blamed on the missing peace officers. Given a chance, Mayor Galt could voice his disapproval and dissatisfaction. The soft-shells would then have a lever to use against Mansfield.

"I reckon you boys can hold the town down while I'm away," Dusty said as Mark finished the explanation.

"If they can't after all you've taught 'em, they're a sorrier bunch than I figured," Calamity commented.

Wilson had been listening in silence and thinking about other things he had heard since his arrival in town. Sucking in his breath, he moved forward.

"From what folks tell me, you're doing something that needs doing bad," the old man said. "If helping me's going to spoil things for you, Cap'n Fog, I say forget it. I'll see what the county sheriff can do."

If anything, the words served to clinch Dusty's determination. Placing the affair in the hands of the county sheriff was not the answer. Before that official, more politician than active peace officer, decided on a course of action, the gang might be across the State line and beyond his jurisdiction. Every instinct Dusty possessed warned that time was of importance in recovering the properties acquired by the Mid-Western Land Syndicate.

"Thanks, Tom," Dusty said, holding out his hand. "Only I reckon I can tend to it. If this bunch can't hold down the town for three-four days, the OD Connected's been wasting money feeding them for a fair spell."

"You're not riding on your lonesome!" the Kid snarled. "I'm coming."

"Waco, Doc and me can handle things here without having any danged Injun underfoot," Mark declared.

"Fact being," Waco went on, "we'll do even better happen you take that baby-faced *Pehnane* with you."

"You boys won't have it any other way?" Dusty asked.

"It's take Lon willing, or we all trail

along," Mark replied and the other two muttered their agreement.

"Trouble being, Lon's not all I need," Dusty said.

"Who else?" Waco inquired hopefully.

"Not you, so simmer down," Dusty answered and looked hard at Calamity. "To make this work, I'll need a wife."

At first the girl did not follow Dusty's meaning. Then she found all the Texans eyeing her with speculative interest and understanding began to creep over her.

"She might just do," Waco commented after a moment.

"And this town's likely to be a whole heap more peaceable happen she's not in it," Mark went on.

"Can't say's how I'd want a mean gal like her for a wife though," the Kid said.

"Just one cottonpicking, chicken-plucking, dod-gasted rebel minute!" Calamity wailed. "What's it all about?"

"It's easy enough, Calam," Dusty explained. "When they reach one of the farms, they'll be talking to me, dressed as a nester and with a wife on hand."

"Me?" the girl asked.

"I'd look like hell in a dress," grinned the Kid.

"You look like hell any which ways!" Calamity snorted. "Me, dressed like—Hey! That means I'll have to wear a dress."

"Reckon you know how to put one on, Calam?" Waco inquired.

"Sure I know how, what d'you reckon I am?"

"Don't you tell her, boy," Mark warned.

"Why I was a regular bridesmaid one time," Calamity stated. "And everybody said how all-fired sweet 'n' lovely I looked in that white gown."

"I reckon we can take it you know how to wear a dress then," Dusty put in. "Funning apart, Calam. I need you. It'll look more natural if there's a woman in the house and I'd rather it's you than the nester's wife if anything goes wrong."

Many women, in view of Dusty's ending words, would have paused to think of the possible consequences of the deception. Worrying about the future, even if it carried the threat of danger, had never been Calamity Jane's way. So she answered without hesitation.

"I allus wanted to marry rich," she

167

grinned. "It's just my stinking luck to wind up hitched to a poor, worthless cuss who's likely to get slickered out of his home."

Indignation creased Lawyer Grosvenor's florid features as he entered the town marshal's office at eight o'clock in the evening. Well-dressed in the latest Eastern style, he had the size and bulk to present an imposing figure. Crossing to the desk, he directed his most forceful glare at Waco who was sitting unconcernedly with his feet elevated on its top.

"I understand that you have two of my clients in the cells, deputy," the lawyer announced.

Slowly the youngster removed his feet and sat up. "Reckon we have," he admitted. "Leastways, they allow to be your clients."

"I'll go in and see them."

"Right now?"

"Yes!" Grosvenor growled. "I've been given to understand that they were arrested this afternoon. Why wasn't I informed sooner?"

"The Kid went to your office to tell you," Waco replied. "Only you wasn't there, so he couldn't."

"My clerk knew where to find me," the lawyer said.

"He wouldn't say, if he did," Waco answered.

Which, in view of the fact that Grosvenor had been involved in some underhand business with a prominent saloon-keeper, did not come entirely as a surprise. Guessing that the Kid had acted under Dusty Fog's orders by not leaving a message with the clerk, Grosvenor became wary. Instead of taking the matter further, he gave a disapproving sniff.

"I'll see Mayor Galt about this later," he warned. "Now can I see my clients?"

"Don't see why not," Waco drawled, not showing any great concern about the threat. "I'll let you in."

Taking Grosvenor into the rear section of the building, Waco unlocked the cell door and allowed him to enter.

"I want to speak with my clients in private," the lawyer said.

"Figured you might," Waco replied, turning the key in the lock. "Yell up when you want to come out."

"You took your own good time coming," Dirk growled.

"I only just learned you'd been arrested," Grosvenor answered, annoyed at the lack of respect. "What happened?"

"We run into one of the fellers we bought a spread off," Dirk replied, aware that Grosvenor knew something of the "buying" methods. "Damned if him and a gal he had along didn't jump us. Afore we could settle 'em, Dusty Fog come and pistol-whipped us down."

Which might not be the exact truth, but Dirk had his pride. He did not wish to admit to a fancy-talking dude law wrangler that it had been a girl who had delivered the *coup de grace* which laid him low.

"So you're being held for assault," Grosvenor said, when Dirk completed the story. "It shouldn't be hard to straighten out. How much have you said?"

"Nothing much. Just that we reckon the old cuss's trying to make out we cheated him so's he can get his farm back and keep the money we paid him for it."

"You'd best stick to that then."

"What if that old bastard talks?" Jigger demanded. "I'd've shut him for good but that big blond deputy near on bust my jaw."

"I thought you said Dusty Fog pistol-whipped you?" Grosvenor said to Dirk.

"Sure it was. There can't be two as big as—"

"Big?" the lawyer repeated.

"Maybe six foot three or more's not big where you come from, mister," Dirk growled. "But for me it'll do until a big feller comes along."

"Six foot thr—" Grosvenor gasped. "That wasn't Dusty Fog, it was Mark Counter. Fog's a short runt who looks like ten cents worth of nothing most of the time."

"But that feller in the office—" Dirk started to say.

Then remembrance struck him and the nagging thought which had caused him so much uneasiness after his interview with "Dusty Fog" became crystal clear. On the street he had noticed the blond giant wore a badge, but it was that of a deputy. Yet the same man undoubtedly sported the insignia of the town's marshal when seated behind the desk in the office. Thinking back, Dirk recalled that at no time had the other Texans referred to the big blond by name.

"You reckon Fog's not very big?" Jigger inquired, cutting in on Dirk's thought train. "I've allus heard—"

"So had I," Grosvenor interrupted testily. "But, you can believe me, he's no more than five foot six at most. You'd take him for the horse wrangler, or cook's louse—"

"We've been took!" Dirk yelped, memory ignited by the lawyer's words.

He remembered the occupant of the adjoining cell, that insignificant cuss he dismissed as being of no importance. Everything began to fall into place. With Mark Counter posing as him, Dusty Fog had occupied the cell, relying upon his unexpected appearance to lull the two prisoners' suspicions.

Realizing how close their escape had been, Dirk felt as if a cold hand touched him. Only his natural caution had made him halt an indiscreet and incriminating conversation. Instead of deputies crouching outside the jail, the listener lay unsuspected in the next cell.

"That tricky son-of-a-bitch!" Grosvenor breathed on hearing Dirk's story. "You're sure you didn't say anything more than you told me?"

"No," Dirk stated. "I saw to that."

"Then things aren't too bad," Grosvenor said. "You'll be fined, nothing more, for the trouble. In fact I'd advise you to plead guilty straight off and get it over. I think I can keep Wilson quiet."

"How?"

"He's been to me for advice. When I leave here, I'll see him and say that if he makes too much of this folks might start thinking you're telling the truth about his motives for attacking you."

"What if he'd told Fog how we got his farm?" Jigger put in.

"Fog's town marshal," Grosvenor replied. "He can't do anything beyond the city limits. With that bill-of-sale you brought in, it's your word against Wilson's about what happened."

"How soon can you get us out of here?" Dirk demanded.

"I don't know if the judge will allow you out on bail," Grosvenor answered. "And it may be best for you to stay put for tonight. Deputy!"

"You through?" Waco inquired, appearing at the connecting door.

"Yes. Where's Captain Fog?"

"Off watch."

"Where can I find him?"

"I never asked," Waco admitted, opening the cell door. "Figured if I did, ole Dusty'd reckon I was nosey and wanted to know."

"Then where's Counter?" Grosvenor growled.

"Who?"

"*Mark* Counter. He's first deputy, isn't he?"

"Mark's making the rounds," the youngster drawled, securing the cell after the lawyer emerged. "And, afore you ask, I'm not sure off hand where he'd be."

"Tell him I'll be back later," Grosvenor snapped and stamped from the passage.

"You boys get the feeling he don't like me too much?" Waco inquired of the prisoners, his voice suggesting the impossibility of such a thing.

An hour passed and the lawyer returned to find Waco still alone in the office. Mark and Doc were keeping up a constant patrol of the town, letting themselves be seen, and ready to nip trouble in the bud before it could blossom.

"I've come to see my clients again," the lawyer said.

"Feel free," Waco replied and led the way into the cell area.

"Hey!" Jigger called as the youngster appeared. "Where's our food?"

"I'll have one of my *amigos* go fetch it when they come in from the rounds," Waco promised. "Got your law wrangler here again."

"Something's come up," Grosvenor told the men after Waco had returned to the office. "Fog, the Ysabel Kid and Calamity Jane rode out just before sundown."

"Calamity Ja—" Dirk spat out. "So that's who she was. Where've they gone?"

"Wilson said to get proof that he'd been swindled. After I left you, I sent for him to come and see me. He looked so bucked up that I knew something was up. So I told him about making a fuss over the attack being prejudicial to his case for regaining his land. He just chuckled and said he'd no more worries over that."

"Why?" Jigger interjected.

"He was a touch coy about it at first, asked me how come I was representing you and took his money as well—"

"I'd say the feller'd got a right smart point there," Dirk commented dryly.

"I told him that you only came to see me for advice on handling the transfer of the property," Grosvenor replied, holding down his indignation. "Then I said I was uneasy about your side of the transaction and intended to find out if there was any truth in his allegations before doing more business with you. That was when I learned why he looked so pleased with himself."

"Why?" Dirk asked, no longer eyeing the lawyer with thinly veiled contempt.

"It seems Fog worked out where your bunch would be 'buying' from something he heard in the cells," Grosvenor told him, a malicious glint in his eyes.

"You stupid—!" Dirk snarled, swinging to face Jigger.

"Hell, Dirk!" The other yelped. "All I said was the boss headed north—And if they've gone north, they'll never find him."

"Don't start fighting between yourselves," Grosvenor warned. "Fog worked it out from a map."

"How'll this affect us?' Dirk demanded.

"The position is much the same," Grosvenor stated. "The bills-of-sale will hold up—unless Fog can prove they were obtained by trickery."

"Can he do it?" Jigger asked.

"Only one way. Apparently he plans to be waiting at a farm, dressed as its owner, and let Stubel 'buy' the place from him."

"The boss'd never fall for it!" Jigger snorted, but Dirk made no comment.

"Fog took you pair in," Grosvenor reminded them. "And he won't be dressed as a Texas cowhand, but in the kind of clothes a nester would wear. I think he might get away with it."

"And if he does," Dirk said quietly, "where's that leave us?"

"In the cell here," Grosvenor answered. "I saw the judge and he's going to accept Fog's suggestion that you are held pending investigations into more serious allegations."

"Can't you square the judge?" Dirk inquired. "I thought this was an easy town."

"Not any more," Grosvenor answered bitterly. "Everything's changed since Mansfield brought Fog in to run the law."

"Hey!" Jigger yelped. "You said Fog's town marshal and can't do anything outside Trail End."

"Not officially," agreed Grosvenor. "But he can make a citizen's arrest if he catches Stubel committing a crime."

"Is that the legal law?" Jigger asked.

"It is," the lawyer confirmed.

"Well I'll swan!" Jigger breathed.

"If Fog gets the proof," Grosvenor went

on, "you pair will face something more serious than a charge of assault."

Silence fell on the cell as its occupants digested the information. While Jigger knew that things had gone wrong, he lacked the intelligence to decide how they might be righted. So he left that part to Dirk and the law wrangler, being ready to go along with whatever they suggested.

Sitting on his bunk, Dirk scowled and thought fast. While the penalty for assault was unlikely to exceed a fine, no such leniency could be expected over the land swindle. Every man concerned in that would face a stiff jail sentence. Knowing something of conditions in the State penitentiary, he did not wish to find himself behind its grim walls.

On learning of Dusty Fog's plan, Grosvenor saw danger to himself in it. If the affair came before the court, his part might be regarded as questionable. Taking money from two clients, on opposing sides of an action, was hardly fair legal practice. With the new, tight administration at the State's capitol, he wished to avoid a close scrutiny of his affairs. Such things had a habit of escalating when disappointed former clients unearthed their grievances.

While aware of its dishonest nature, Grosvenor wanted Stubel's money too much to turn his business away. Since Dusty Fog's arrival in Trail End there had been an alarming reduction in the lawyer's sources of income, with the threats of even greater cuts to come unless the small Texan could speedily be removed from office.

Learning of Dusty's secret departure, Grosvenor saw a way the removal might be caused. If something happened—a jail escape with the life of a prominent citizen endangered for example—Mayor Galt could use it as an excuse to request the Texan's dismissal. There were a number of influential politicians who would back up the demand without regard for the reasons causing Dusty Fog's absence.

So Grosvenor had brought the means of a chance of escape with him. After priming them with his words, he went on with his scheme. If he judged the two men correctly, they would leap at any opportunity to avoid facing a trial.

"I thought you had the right to know how things stand," he said, shoving back his jacket to place his hands on his hips as he turned towards the door of the cell and raised his voice. "I'm all through now, deputy!"

Looking up, Dirk stiffened slightly. In moving back the skirts of his jacket, the lawyer had exposed the butt of a Merwin & Hulbert revolver in his hip pocket. Coming to his feet as the connecting door opened, Dirk caught Grosvenor's arm with one hand and with the other drew the revolver. Moving his hands, Grosvenor allowed the jacket to fall back into position and gave no sign that he knew of the revolver's departure.

"You want to come out, Mr. Grosvenor?" Waco inquired as he entered.

"No," Dirk replied, cocking the revolver and pressing its muzzle against the lawyer's head. "*We* want out. Open up, or you'll have one real dead law wrangler."

A cold chill of apprehension flooded over Grosvenor as he realized his life hung in the young Texan's hands. Yet he did not need to worry. While Waco regarded the lawyer with justifiable contempt, his sense of duty prevented him from doing anything that might endanger the other. Equally Waco knew he must try to prevent the escape. With their combined knowledge, Mark, Doc and

Waco could keep the town peaceful until Dusty's return. However an escape from the jail would be all Mayor Galt and the others needed to make demands that Mansfield remove Dusty from office.

Slowly Waco walked towards the cell door. Alert for any opportunity, he studied the men with extra interest. Dirk was the one to watch, fast, deadly, willing to kill without hesitation. There could be no taking reckless chances with such a man. Nor could Waco expect help from Grosvenor. Whether the lawyer knew anything about how the gun came into Dirk's hands did not concern the youngster right then. Fear for his life would stop Grosvenor trying to help, even without his being fully aware of the escape's possibilities.

"Do it, deputy!" Grosvenor hissed and the fear in his voice was not entirely assumed.

Walking forward, Waco turned the key in the lock and thrust open the door. At the same time he kept his left hand held well clear of the near side Colt.

"Back off to the wall," Dirk commanded, still keeping the gun to Grosvenor's head. "Then spread your arms out shoulder high and stay put."

Waco obeyed, feeling himself fortunate in that the prisoners had never seen the very efficient way in which Dusty Fog would have handled a similar situation.

Forced to stand facing the wall with legs wide apart and body inclined forward, supported by the palms of the hands, he could have done nothing against the men.

"Where's our guns, kid?" Jigger demanded, walking from the cell.

"Locked in the safe and Mark's got the key," Waco replied. "I'll go ask him for it if you like."

"Get his guns, Jigger!" Dirk snapped, shoving Grosvenor through the door but still pressing the Merwin & Hulbert's .45 nose against the lawyer's skull. "We'll go out the back door."

"You do just that," Waco grinned. "Ole Pappy Wilson and the gal's out there. Way I heard it, they licked you good in the street."

Just as Waco hoped, Jigger took the bait. Anger at the thought of how he had come to be arrested, mingled with a combined antipathy for Texans and peace officers, caused him to draw back his right arm.

"You've got a real big mouth, boy!" Jigger

snarled, shooting his fist at Waco's face even as Dirk prepared to yell a warning.

Born with lightning fast reactions, which the life he led did nothing to reduce, Waco moved with all his speed. At the last moment he jerked his head aside, allowing Jigger's fist to fly by and strike the wall behind him. Across the passage, Dirk started to turn the gun from Grosvenor. With a heave, the lawyer tore free from the hardcase's hand and sprang away. Expecting no trouble from that quarter, Dirk concentrated on Waco.

Everything happened at almost blinding speed. Even as pain knifed into Jigger, Waco's right hand came across to catch his shoulder and shove. At the same moment the youngster's left hand flashed downwards, fingers reaching for the staghorn handle of the waiting Colt. Jigger staggered away, leaving Waco exposed to Dirk's weapon. Steel rasped on leather as Waco's Colt cleared the holster lip, cocked and lining instinctively. His finger squeezed the trigger and thumb released the hammer.

Two factors combined to save Waco: his own speed and the limitations of the Merwin & Hulbert Army Pocket revolver. Designed with a three-and-a-half inch barrel for ease of concealment, the gun felt vastly different from the Colt to which Dirk had become accustomed. So he found difficulty in altering his aim and the double action mechanism added to his downfall. With the hammer drawn back to full cock, the pressure needed to fire was less than on a single action Colt in the same position. Before Dirk completed his alteration of direction, he squeezed just a shade more than he intended with his forefinger. Not enough to set off a Colt, but sufficient for the Merwin & Hulbert. It barked and the bullet slapped into the wall at Waco's side.

An instant later the youngster's Colt crashed. Waco shot to kill, knowing no other way would stop a man like Dirk. Caught in the left side of the chest, Dirk rocked backwards and the revolver flew from his fingers. It clattered to the floor, sliding along towards Jigger's feet.

Seeing the escape attempt start to go wrong, Grosvenor reached a rapid decision. Neither of the prisoners must be recaptured alive and able to tell where the Merwin & Hulbert had come from. A glance showed him that Waco had ended that danger in Dirk's case; which still left Jigger. Although the revolver lay almost at his feet, he might not try to pick it up. Even if he should try, Waco could stop him without needing to kill.

Aware of the consequences should Jigger live and talk, Grosvenor acted. The revolver had not been the lawyer's only weapon. Slipping a Remington Double Derringer from his jacket he cut loose with both barrels and the bullets tore into Jigger's head. Not yet recovered from Waco's shove, the hard-case toppled over to the floor.

From turning to face Jigger, Waco swung in Grosvenor's direction. The youngster turned ready to shoot but the sight of the lawyer's weapon told him there would be no need.

"Where did he get the gun?" Waco demanded.

Before any more could be said, the office's outer door burst open and feet thudded fast towards the cells. Guns in hand, Mark and Doc burst into the passage.

"What happened?" Mark asked, eyes taking in the scene.

"Get to that one, Doc!" Waco snapped, indicating Dirk, then looked at Mark. "They got hold of a gun somewheres. Held it on the law wrangler and told me to open up. I did it."

"You'd no other choice but to," Mark stated, fixing Grosvenor with his cold stare. "Had he, Counsellor?"

Only for a moment did Grosvenor pause, for he read cold menace in the blond giant's blue eyes. Already more men were making their appearance at the connecting door, Trail End citizens eager to learn what had happened. There might be a chance to cast doubts on the Texan's efficiency, but Grosvenor declined to try.

"None at all," the lawyer answered, conscious that his words would be repeated around the town.

"This one's dead," Doc reported, to Grosvenor's relief. "Where in hell did the gun come from?"

"Passed through the window during the evening by a confederate, possibly," Grosvenor suggested, watching as Doc approached the second body. "Is he—?"

"Deader'n the other one," Doc replied.

"I had to do it," Grosvenor said. "He could have had a gun like the other man."

"You'd got a gun with you?" Doc growled.

"I always carry one. It's lucky for your friend I had it this time."

"Likely I could've stopped him," Waco put in.

"And if you hadn't?" Grosvenor replied. "I daren't take that chance."

For once the man told the truth, although not in the way the listeners accepted his meaning. Before Mark could comment on the statement, one of the on-lookers asked the question Grosvenor hoped to hear.

"Where's Cap'n Fog?"

"Out of town," Waco answered, ahead of Mark's intention to make an evasive reply. "Maybe you gents heard about old Tom Wilson getting slickered out of his place?" A murmur of agreement came and the youngster continued, "Dusty figured to fetch in the jaspers who did it."

"Good for him!" put in another of the small crowd and that appeared to be the general opinion.

"Doc," Mark said. "Get the bodies to the undertaker, these gents'll help you. I want to talk to you, Counsellor."

"I'm at your disposal," Grosvenor replied. Yet for all that the lawyer felt uneasy as he watched the removal of the bodies and departure of the on-lookers. At a sign from Mark, Waco closed the connecting door. Then they faced Grosvenor, menace in their relaxed postures.

"How d'you reckon they got that gun, Counsellor?" Mark began.

"I can only repeat what I said before—" Grosvenor replied.

"Reckon we could find out who-all owns it?" Waco put in, holding the Merwin & Hulbert which he had picked up during the removal of the bodies. "Can't be all that many of 'em around."

"That's good thinking," Grosvenor complimented, satisfied that the revolver could not be traced back to him.

"Why do you reckon they tried to bust out all of a sudden, Counsellor?" Mark inquired.

"From what they said," Grosvenor replied, using the words thought out since the shooting, "they'd learned somehow of Captain Fog's departure. Possibly the man who gave them the gun told them."

"That's *real* likely," Waco said dryly.

"They seemed worried about the consequences if he learned the truth," Grosvenor went on. "I'm pleased that I discovered in time what they were up to. Their employer wanted me to act for him."

"Did you?" Mark asked.

"Only in a minor capacity. Of course when I heard two of his men had been arrested, I considered it my duty to learn why or if there was any foundation to Mr. Wilson's allegations."

"Was there?"

"They insisted the bills-of-sale had been obtained legally and suggested Mr. Wilson was pretending they cheated him to get his place back and keep the payment. Now, in view of what has happened, I think he told the truth."

"I want a written statement of all you've told me," Mark said. "Including that you don't hold Waco, or any member of the marshal's office, responsible for the escape try. And that you figure, with you in their hands, that Waco acted for the best all through."

Once more two pairs of eyes locked, but Grosvenor looked away first. He did not know how much the Texans suspected, or could prove, so decided he must yield to the blond giant's demands.

"I'll do that," the lawyer promised.

"Now's as good a time as any," Mark told him. "There's a pen and paper on the desk, and everything's still fresh in your mind."

"Very well," Grosvenor sighed.

"Go get two gents to witness it, boy," Mark continued.

"I'll pick 'em special," grinned the youngster and left.

On his return, Waco proved to have kept his word. Grosvenor knew that the two men accompanying the youngster gave whole-hearted support to Dusty Fog's efforts at cleaning up the town. With their names on the paper, the lawyer could not disavow the statement at a later date.

"Well," Mark said after the lawyer and witnesses had left the office. "How about his story?"

"It could be true," Waco replied. "Or he either took in the gun, or had it passed through the window to them. Damn it! I should've searched him afore I let him go in."

"Likely none of us would've, boy. You did the right thing telling them fellers about Dusty going after that bunch."

"Figured it'd come out anyways," Waco drawled. "So I allowed it'd be best if we did the telling. Do we let him get away with it, Mark?"

"For now. There's nothing we can hold against him. Maybe he told them about Dusty going after the rest of the bunch, but we can't prove it."

"How'll folks feel about Dusty up and pulling out that ways?"

"Most of 'em'll allow he's doing the right thing," Mark answered. "As long as he brings Stubel's bunch in and proves what they've been doing."

"Tired, Calam?" Dusty asked gently as he and the girl sat their leg-weary horses and waited for the Kid to return from the rim overlooking the Deccan River.

"A mite," she replied. "I know now why us Yankees never caught you in Arkansas."

"They might have, if they'd had riders as good as you along," Dusty praised.

"You're only saying that 'cause it's true," Calamity said, grinning wryly.

During the War, the Texas Light Cavalry and in particular Dusty's company had built a reputation for hard, fast riding which won the grudging admiration of their enemies. On the journey from Trail End, Calamity had formed an impression of the way that reputation had been won. Leaving the town shortly after sun-down, riding a three horse relay, Dusty, the Kid and Calamity had made good time. Halting for only a short time during the night, they had approached the Deccan Valley shortly before noon. Calamity would never forget that ride and it said much for her ability on a horse that she had avoided delaying them.

"They're at that place over the rim now," reported the Kid, returning from scouting the land ahead.

"Let's go get 'em!" Calamity suggested eagerly.

"We'll play it the way I said," Dusty replied.

"She just don't want to wear that dress," grinned the Kid.

"Danged Injun!" Calamity sniffed. "Anyways, I don't see why we can't jump 'em right here 'n' now."

"Because there're folks in that house, hothead, is why," Dusty answered. "I don't aim to get them hurt, which could happen. We'll go to the next place and wait."

For a moment Calamity sat looking around. In the course of her work, she had travelled through the Deccan Valley several times and knew most of its occupants. So she thought fast and figured out who owned the next farm.

"Damn the luck!" she snorted.

"What's up, Calam?" inquired the Kid.

"That'll be Jack Hudson's place. He don't like Texans."

"Maybe he won't know we're Texans," grinned the Kid.

"Yah!" Calamity scoffed, studying their clothing which spelled TEXAN to anybody who knew "sic 'em" about the West. "He'd know it even afore you start yelling. 'Remember the Alamo'."

"We'll go see him anyways," Dusty decided. "Do you know him, Calam?"

"Him and his missus both. Which they've got good taste, they like me—'course I'm no Texan."

"And the good Sovereign State of Texas sings 'Lordy, hallelujah!' for that," the Kid told her. "Let's go see this Hudson gent."

With Calamity telling the Kid in pungent, hide-searing terms what she thought of him and the Sovereign State of Texas, the trio turned their horses westwards. Being uncertain of how much time they had before the gang's arrival, Dusty set a fast pace. At last, after covering almost two miles, Calamity swung her horse towards the top of the rim.

"Be about level with 'em now," she told her companions.

"Reckon those jaspers could've licked us here, Lon?" Dusty asked.

"Don't see it," the Kid replied. "Three of them was just going into the house with Stubel and the farmer when I looked over. Anyways, Stubel's riding a buggy and couldn't travel as fast as we just did."

"You'd best take a look before we show ourselves," Dusty ordered. "We don't want to scare them off."

Advancing, the Kid peered over the skyline. Below him lay a section of the Deccan Valley, with the river curling along it. He studied the small log cabin, outbuildings and cultivated land of a well maintained farm, but saw no sign of Stubel's party. Then his eyes raked the surrounding area in search of hidden watchers. Satisfied that the gang had not sent a man ahead, he signalled Calamity and Dusty to join him.

"If there's one of 'em around, he's a better Injun than me," the Kid stated.

Going over the rim and down towards the valley floor, Dusty decided his theory on the gang's activities was correct. Along most of its course, the Deccan River tended to lie close to the northern side of the valley. The land in the valley bottom could not be classed as productive compared with the surrounding districts. Lastly, the valley offered an open, unbroken route to the north west. Any railroad thinking of running tracks in that direction would be likely to select the Deccan Valley as the most suitable right-of-way. In which case, the farms along it would be valuable properties. The railroad would need to buy them from the owners before being able to lay the tracks over the land.

A man and woman emerged from the log cabin as the trio drew closer, taking Dusty's thoughts from his theories. While riding towards them, Dusty studied the couple. In his late twenties, the man had red hair, a ruggedly handsome face and well-developed body. Dressed in the style of a working farmer, he scowled at the Texans. By his side, the woman wore an old gingham dress, had mouse brown hair and a pretty face. About Calamity's size, she looked the kind who would enjoy having company but seemed perturbed rather than pleased at the sight of the visitors. Laying a hand on the man's arm, she spoke quietly to him. From her attitude, Dusty concluded that she was giving a warning of some kind.

Following the dictates of range-country etiquette, the trio halted their horses before the farmer and his wife but did not dismount. A faint smile, tinged just a little with relief, played around the woman's lips at the sight of Calamity. However the man's face stayed truculently watchful as he eyed the Texans.

"Howdy, Susie, Jack," Calamity greeted.

"Hi, Calam," the woman answered when her husband did not speak.

"Been in the saddle a fair spell, Jack," Calamity hinted.

"Light and rest yourself," Hudson said grudgingly.

"This here's Cap'n Dusty Fog and the Ysabel Kid from down Trail End way," the girl announced, swinging from the back of her lathered horse. "We've come out here to help you."

"Ag'in what?" Hudson grunted, making no attempt to acknowledge the introduction.

"A bunch of land-grabbing skunks who're taking farms from folk all along the Deccan,"

Calamity replied, an irritated edge creeping into her voice. "Tell 'em about it, Cap'n Dusty."

Quickly Dusty told the Hudsons what he knew. While interested, and displeased with what he heard, the young farmer could not shake off his suspicions and antipathy where Texans were concerned.

"You reckon they only take from folks who can't read and write," he said. "Maybe you reckon none of us farmers can. Well, I read and write real good."

"Then *you've* nothing to worry over," Dusty replied. "How about the folks on the place back there to the east, or your neighbours along to the west?"

"Gus Strange up there'd likely not know enough to figure he's been slickered," Calamity pointed out.

"Maybe I'll stop that bunch right here!" Hudson snapped, tapping the butt of the 1860 Army Colt thrust into his waistband.

"Jack!" Susie Hudson gasped.

"Mister," growled the Kid, face Comanche-mean as he moved ahead of his friends. His right hand twisted palm out, coiled around the worn walnut grips of the Old Dragoon and slid it from leather. "I don't know how good you are. But unless you're a whole heap faster'n that, I'd say you should leave it to us."

Hudson took an involuntary pace to the rear as he stared into the muzzle of the old Colt. Then the gun turned on the Kid's finger and dropped back into leather. Anger flushed Hudson's face and he opened his mouth to say something.

"Danged fool Comanche!" Calamity spat out. "Only he's right for once in his sinful life. Jack, I've seen two of this bunch. If the rest're's good, you'd be dead afore you touched that gun."

"That was a damned fool trick!" Hudson spat out. "Just about what I'd expect from a cowhand."

"I never saw a sod-buster with sense enough to pack sand into a rat-hole, comes to that," the Kid bristled back.

"Easy, Lon. What're you getting riled about, you're no cowhand," Dusty said and looked at the farmer. "Mister, Calamity isn't funning about that bunch."

"So I'll look after my own!" Hudson growled.

"And how about the other folks?" Dusty

asked. "The ones who've lost their places already?"

"The law'll get them back—!" Hudson began.

"Not the way that gang's worked it," Dusty interrupted.

"So I'll get the other farmers together and we'll take 'em back!" Hudson yelled. "We don't need no help from bee—"

At which point Miss Canary took a hand. Never one to suffer plumb foolishness gladly, she had been growing increasingly indignant at the male bickering. So she decided the time had come for female good sense to take control.

"For land's sake, Susie, talk some sense into that fool husband of your'n's head. I didn't ride my pants see-through thin and butt end to a frazzle to hear the men-folks whittle-whanging about who's best out of cowhands and nesters."

"This here's my home—!" Hudson protested.

It seemed to be his day for having noble, profound speeches cut off short. Hot with indignation at her husband's display of bad manners before the visitors, Susie forgot that a wife should remain meekly in the background at such a time. Catching hold of her husband's arm, she swung him to face her.

"It's my home too, Jack Hudson!" she yelled. "These folks've been good enough to come out from Trail End to warn us—and look like they've rode mighty hard to do it. The least you can do is hear them out."

Only rarely did Susie stop being a loyal and dutiful wife, but when she did Jack Hudson found himself wishing things were back to normal. So, like many another wise married man, he decided to forget his prejudices in the interests of retaining a happy home.

"All right," he said. "Let's hear it."

"There's nobody like us women-folk for talking good sense," grinned Calamity.

"Go keep watch on the east trail, Lon," Dusty ordered, ignoring the comment. "I want to let this bunch sell *me* your place, Mr. Hudson."

"You?" the farmer snorted.

"Sure. That way we'll have proof of their game."

"You aim to be in the house, dressed like a farmer and without your guns?" Hudson growled after Dusty had explained the plan.

"That's just how we fix to do it," the small Texan agreed.

"What if they suspicion you?"

"I'll try not to let them do too much damage to your place."

"With your bare hands?" Hudson asked.

"If I have to," Dusty agreed, guessing what troubled the other man.

"A shor—A feller your size?"

"Do you reckon you could stop a feller my size walking by you and into the house, Mr. Hudson?"

"Without guns?"

"Without guns," Dusty answered, starting to unbuckle his belt.

"I reckon I just could," Hudson stated.

With a groan of anguish Calamity clapped a hand to her forehead and raised her eyes to the sky.

"Lordy lord!" she said piously. "Apart from Cap'n Dusty, I never yet saw a man with one lick of good sense until he got it knocked into his fool head."

"Stop them, Calam!" Susie gasped, knowing her husband's feeling where Texas cowboys were concerned and studying the difference in their sizes.

"Shuckens," Calamity grinned. "I don't reckon Cap'n Dusty'll hurt him."

Handing his gunbelt to the girl, Dusty

walked in the direction of the house. Surprised to find his challenge accepted so promptly, Hudson stood and stared for a moment. Then annoyance filled him. If that short-grown beef-head reckoned to make a fool out of Jack Hudson, he was going to wish the idea never came his way. With that thought in mind, Hudson launched himself forward. His big hands reached towards Dusty, ready to grab hold. If Hudson gave the matter any thought, he probably expected Dusty to step back, or go sideways in an attempt to avoid being caught. Instead the small Texan came to meet him.

The unexpected action took Hudson off balance and he did not find time to recover. Going forward, Dusty passed between the farmer's hands. Before they could close on him, he started to turn around. Swiftly Dusty's right hand rose, going across the front of Hudson's left shoulder to grip the back of his shirt's collar. At the same time Dusty's other hand caught the man's right elbow. Completing his turn, the small Texan bowed his legs slightly and bent his torso forward. Tugging at the trapped elbow and thrusting forward on the collar, he caused Hudson to pass helplessly over his side.

Letting out a squawl of surprise, the farmer found himself turned in the air and dumped on to his back. Nor did his troubles end there. To prevent the other from landing too hard, Dusty went down with him. Settling on his rump facing towards Hudson's head on his left side, Dusty brought his hand from the collar. Before Hudson could recover his scattered wits, Dusty placed his bent left arm on the farmer's chest. Then Dusty's right arm curled over and beneath the other man's left bicep to trap the limb against his side. At first the farmer tried to struggle, but the pressure on his chest and leverage against his arm held him helpless.

Not wishing to embarrass the young farmer further in front of the women, Dusty released his holds and stood up. Bending down, he helped the farmer rise.

"Sorry about that, friend," Dusty said. "I just went right on with it instead of quitting after the throw."

Figuring the affair to be at an end, with his point made, Dusty turned to see if the Kid was giving any sign of sighting the gang. Face flushed with annoyance, Hudson lunged forward. Catching Dusty's right wrist in his left hand, he bent the arm behind the small

Texan's back and gripped its bicep with his other hand. For the first time Hudson started to be aware of Dusty's strength as he felt the size of the muscle under his fingers. However the realization had not fully sunk in as he began to ask.

"What'll you do i—"

Without waiting for the full question, Dusty supplied its answer. Leaning backwards instead of struggling and pulling away, he went swiftly to work at freeing himself. Up and around whipped Dusty's left arm, passing over Hudson's right then down to take hold of the farmer's left wrist. A startled grunt broke from Hudson as he found his arms trapped. Pivoting on his right foot, Dusty swung his left leg to strike against his attacker's shins. Hudson could not save himself as Dusty applied pressure on his trapped right arm. Once more he felt his feet leave the ground and he whirled over to land with sufficient force to jolt most of the breath from his body.

"Jack!" Susie yelled, flinging herself to her husband's side.

"Now maybe you pair'll quit horsing around," Calamity said unsympathetically.

"I hate like hell to be a spoilsport, but them fellers'll be coming sometime soon."

Slowly and painfully Hudson eased himself into a sitting position. A glimmer of respect crept unwillingly into his face as he looked at Dusty.

"I don't know how the hell you did it, but you did," Hudson muttered. "Reckon you've made your point. Do what you have to do."

"Move it, Calam," Dusty commanded, bending to help Hudson stand up. "Get the gear from the saddlebags."

"Ease off there," she replied. "You're beginning to sound like a husband."

At that moment the Kid returned. Sliding his horse to a halt, he jerked a thumb over his shoulder.

"They're coming, Dusty. 'Bout a mile off and not hurrying."

"We'll hide in the barn," Hudson suggested.

"No," Dusty replied. "They may nose around, or hear the horses. Best go down by the river."

"I know a place," the farmer said. "Let's get to it."

"Looks like he got convinced," the Kid whispered to Calamity as he went to collect the horses.

"If that husband of mine'd teach me all them fancy tricks," Calamity replied, holding a bundle of clothes taken from the saddlebags, "I'd never have to worry about getting licked by another gal."

"Ask him nice while you're tending his needs all loving, and he might," advised the Kid. "Say, I can't wait to see you all fancied up."

Taking the horses' reins, he led them away before Calamity could reply. Which, in view of what she said, was probably just as well.

A feeling of well-being and contentment filled Joshua Stubel as he drove his buggy to the next farm along the Deccan Valley. If he should obtain it, he could send one of his escort into Trail End with a further eight bills-of-sale. That would only leave three of the boys along with him, so he decided the next place would be his last acquisition. Anyway, he could waste no more time dickering with dumb rural hicks if he hoped to reach Sharon Springs by the following Monday.

Reaching that town was important. Wishing to avoid attracting attention to its plans, the railroad company had decided to send its land buyer from West Kansas instead of out of its eastern headquarters. Stubel planned to meet the man at Sharon Springs and sell him the properties acquired along the Deccan Valley. At the price Stubel intended to ask, the land buyer would be only too willing to accept the places. Once that happened, the chubby, pleasant-featured trickster figured the railroad and the real owners could settle their own problems. For his part, he would be headed west as fast as he could travel.

When the farm came into sight, Stubel gazed at it with detached interest. He wished that dumb Swede, Strange, back at the previous place had been able to tell him more about the Hudsons. However Strange spoke little English and Stubel did not feel like taking added time to gather details which could be picked up easier at first hand. Salty, Lip, Chambers and Dobley ought to be able to handle any fuss if it started. Especially if it came from the short runt who walked out of the cabin and looked their way.

"Dog-blasted fool outfit!" Calamity sniffed, eyeing with disgust the gingham dress she was wearing over her shirt and pants. "Why in hell do women wear such do-dads?"

"Most women likely think that about the way you dress," Dusty replied.

"What's wrong with the way I dress?" the girl demanded belligerently.

"Not a thing," Dusty grinned. "I love you no matter what you wear. Now go stir the stew afore it sticks to the bottom of the pot."

Making a hurried dart across the room, Calamity obeyed the order. They were in the cabin's combined kitchen and dining-room, where the girl had just finished packing away everything breakable in case of trouble. Reaching the stove, she stirred a pot of stew which was bubbling on its top.

"Hope the boys're holding the town down," she remarked, glancing to make sure that the towel covered her Colt on the table by the stove.

"I reckon they ca—" Dusty began and looked out of the window. "Here they come, Calam!"

"Got your gun handy?"

"It's on the side-piece, under Jack's hat. Don't let them see that smoke-pole of yours unless it's needed. I'm going out there to meet them. It'll be interesting to see how they make their play."

Walking from the cabin, Dusty darted a quick glance around. He could see nothing to arouse the gang's suspicions. That figured. Trust the Kid to make sure that the Hudsons and their horses were well out of sight. Satisfied on that score, Dusty turned his attention to the approaching men. To his relief, he saw that none of the four men riding around the buggy equalled the quality of the jasper Calamity had clubbed down in Trail End. Wearing range clothes and low-hanging guns, they looked to be an average bunch of hired hard-cases such as could be gathered in any big Western town.

From the riders, Dusty looked at the buggy's occupant. Middle-sized, well-padded, Stubel wore a sober black suit, round topped hat and exuded an air of geniality which would disarm most people. Yet, on bringing the harness horse to a halt, he hopped from the driving seat with a rubbery agility which did not go unnoticed by the small Texan.

"Good afternoon, young man," Stubel greeted, taking a long envelope from his inside pocket as he walked towards Dusty. "Can you tell me where this is?"

"Ain't no hand at reading," Dusty answered. "Missus's inside, but she don't read none neither."

"A pity. A great pity," Stubel said. "Is this your place?"

"Sure is. Got it offen my uncle just recent. He passed on sudden-like."

"And the title is in your name?"

"So the lawyer told me."

"I'm afraid I've got some disturbing news for you," Stubel warned, removing a sheet of paper from the envelope and opening it out. "This is my authority as official land-buyer for the United States Army."

"Sure looks like it might be," Dusty admitted, peering in an uncomprehending manner at the official-appearing printing which would have verified Stubel's claim had it been genuine. Clearly the man was taking no chance of being caught out by a victim pretending to be illiterate when able to read. "What you want with me?"

"I'm sorry to have to tell you this," Stubel said, and sounded it. "But the Army is to build a fort on this piece of land here and I've been sent to buy it."

"What iffen I don't want to sell?" Dusty asked.

"I'm afraid you've no choice," the chubby man replied smoothly. "We have to put the fort here and the Government says that you must sell the land to us for that purpose. However, I'm here to do the right thing by you."

Dusty stood for a moment, scratching his head and looking around in a perplexed manner which he hoped would be right. Apparently the men suspected nothing, so he gave a despairing shrug.

"Reckon I've no choice then?"

"None at all, young man," Stubel agreed. "However, have no fear. The Government will reimburse you for the loss of your home."

"Gee!" Dusty gasped. "And will they pay me for the place as well?"

"Most handsomely, I assure you."

"Come on in the house, mister," Dusty offered. "Reckon we can talk better on our butt ends round the table."

"Thank you, young man," Stubel replied. "I hope you don't mind if these officers of the law accompany me? We need witnesses to protect your interests as well as my own."

"Shuckens no!" Dusty answered, wondering if he might be overplaying the part. However the men still appeared to accept him as valid, so he continued, "Come on in, gents. My lil wife's done whomped up a mess of stew and you're surely welcome to set in on it."

"Stop outside and keep watch, Salty," Stubel ordered in a low voice as Dusty went into the cabin. "This one's going to be easy."

"Here, lil wife," Dusty called as the men trooped in after him. "Set up victuals for us now."

Darting a glance at the girl, Dusty saw her body stiffen slightly at the name he applied to her. There was going to be pop once Miss Canary found herself free to speak her mind.

Taking a chair at the table's end closest to where his gun lay hidden on the side-piece, Dusty watched Stubel sit opposite him. The chubby trickster had collected an impressive document case from the buggy and laid it before him, unbuckling its fastenings. However none of his companions sat down. Lip and Chambers, a pair of tall, gaunt hard-cases with dark hair and cold eyes, stood on either side of their boss. Crossing to the stove, the shorter, more heavily built Dobley hooked his rump on the table by it and inadvertently, but effectively, blocked Calamity's access to her revolver. Like a dutiful little wife, Calamity carried a plate of stew over and placed it before Dusty.

"I hope it burns your tongue off!" she mouthed, with her back to the men.

"Thanks, lil wife," Dusty replied. "You just get on with your chores and leave us men-folks tend to business."

If ever Calamity found need to exercise her self-control, it was at that moment. Swinging from the table, she returned to the stove and asked if any of the men-folks would like some stew. Despite her annoyance, she managed to sound just like a dutiful little wife attending to her visitors' needs.

"I'll have some, g—missus," Dobley answered, but the rest declined on the grounds of having fed at the last place.

While Calamity filled a plate for Dobley, Dusty waited to see the rest of the swindle. Already he knew one method they used to discover whether their proposed victim could read and admitted it to be effective.

"Now, young man," Stubel said, producing a pen and papers from his case. "While the Government must take your lands, we have no desire to be oppressive or cause you hardship. So I am empowered to pay you the sum of two thousand dollars for your property."

"T-two thousand dollars!" Dusty gurgled.

"Whee-doggie! Did you-all hear that then, lil wife?"

"I heard," Calamity agreed, shoving the stew pot to the edge of the stove. "Why I can buy me a new fancy dress 'n' some high-button shoes—"

"Naturally you won't receive all the money right now," Stubel put in.

"We won't?" Dusty asked.

"No. That's not the way Government deals are made. I needn't explain why to a man of the world like you."

"Reckon not," Dusty answered, acting impressed by the flattery. "How do we get it?"

"Two hundred dollars now," Stubel replied, watching his "victim's" face and ready to add money should he read signs of objection to the price. Seeing none, he continued, "And the rest when you deliver a notice of sale to the Land Office in Mulrooney."

"Mulrooney!" Dusty yelped. "Trail End's a whole heap closer."

"But not the kind of town you'd care to take your charming wife into—"

"We wouldn't be there for long—" Dusty started to say more but Calamity decided to intervene.

"In and out's all," she said. "And more'n enough with that town."

Clearly Stubel had come prepared to deal with any insistence to visit Trail End.

"I agree, my dear young lady," he said in his most winning manner, then leaned towards Dusty in a confiding manner. "This is in the strictest confidence, Mr. Hudson, but it will be to your advantage to go to Mulrooney. The Government is offering some choice sections of farm land for sale near there. If you mention that you lost your home this way, I'm sure you can take first whack at it. The price will be reasonable. I bet you get a better place than this for—well one thousand dollars at most."

"It's Mulrooney for us then," Dusty enthused.

"A word of warning, not that a man of your experience needs it of course," Stubel went on. "If I was you, I wouldn't say a word about this sale, even to any of your neighbours if you meet them on the trail. There's only a limited amount of land offered for sale and it is all very desirable. The less who know, the better your chances of obtaining a section."

"I'll mind it," Dusty promised.

"Here is your two hundred then," Stubel said, counting off the momey from a thick pad taken out of the case. "I'll write a note for the Land Office in Mulrooney, authorizing them to pay the rest of the price to you, and you can sign the bill-of-sale for me."

"I don't write neither," Dusty pointed.

"Your mark, witnessed by U.S. Marshal Chambers here, will be sufficient."

"If it suits you, it suits me."

Sensing that the affair was drawing towards its climax, Calamity sought for a way to reach her gun. To her annoyance, she saw that Dobley's movements on the table had caused the towel to slip. The Colt's ivory butt showed plainly and, although concealed by the man's body, would be in view if he stood up. So she could not ask him to leave the table. Cursing the female garments which prevented her from toting the bull whip, Calamity looked around for some other weapon. Among the cooking utensils hung on pegs along the wall behind the stove was an iron skillet.

"There," thought Calamity, "is what I call real thoughtful of Susie."

With that in mind, she moved along the stove and started to readjust the hanging pots and pans. At the same time she kept her attention on what was being said and done at the dining table.

Producing a pen from his case, Stubel took a small inkpot out of his vest pocket. The note he wrote and passed to Dusty claimed to give J. Hudson the right to collect the sum of eighteen hundred dollars from the Mulrooney Land Office, to complete payment for all title to his property in the Deccan Valley.

Once again Dusty felt impressed with Stubel's efficiency. Written in the correct legal terms, the note might have been genuine and would strike an unsuspecting person who read it as being above board. The ink dried a normal blue-black colour and Dusty wondered how long would elapse before the chemical reaction caused the writing to disappear. Probably not for some hours as Stubel would want as much time as possible before the disappearance was discovered.

"Whatever you do, keep that safe," Stubel warned, handing the paper to Dusty. "Without it, you won't get paid the rest of the sale price."

"I'll take real good care of it," Dusty assured him.

While pretending to concentrate on folding

the paper and putting it into his pocket, Dusty surreptitiously watched the chubby man. Swiftly Stubel scooped the inkpot into his case and brought out another identical in appearance. That told Dusty how the ink on the letter disappeared, but not that upon the bill-of-sale.

"And now, Mr. Hudson," Stubel said, placing three papers before Dusty in a neat pile. "If you will sign these. They are the bill-of-sale for your farm."

"I'm only getting paid the once," Dusty protested.

"Of course. But these others are copies of the transaction. One for the Army, showing they have right to build. One for the Land Office and the other for my own department. If you wish, I'll read out what the papers say."

"Go to it," Dusty said.

As Dusty expected, the legal terms sounded authentic. In fact they were such as would be used in a legitimate document by which the United States Army might purchase Hudson's property.

"The other two are exact copies of this one," Stubel finished, passing the papers across the table.

While that proved to be true of the second sheet, as Dusty found on signing the first and passing it to the waiting Chambers, the third of the papers contained two major differences. Instead of the buyer being the United States Army, the name given was the Mid-Western Land Syndicate. Also the third paper stated that the price had been paid in full. Showing no sign that he had noticed the differences, Dusty used the pen again and pushed the paper to Chambers.

Being a sufferer from haemorrhoids, Dobley found difficulty in sitting still on the hard top of the table. Wriggling his rump in an effort to ease the discomfort, he put down the empty plate. Feeling something hard against the seat of his pants, he reached behind to touch a familiar object and picked it up.

The fact that there was a revolver in the house aroused no comment. Even its being hidden on the table could be put down to no more than a precaution taken until the callers had shown their intentions. So Dobley thought nothing of the matter until he actually saw Calamity's gun. A rechambered Navy Colt with an ivory butt and Best Citizen's finish seemed out of place in the home of a poor young farmer.

At the same moment that Dobley opened his mouth to mention the find, Chambers also made a discovery. Shoving aside the first two papers, having witnessed the mark made by their "victim", he reached for the third and most important page. For a moment he failed to realize what made it different from its predecessors. Then, with a sense of shock, he saw that the words, "D.E.M. Fog" stood out where a simple cross should be.

"What the—!" Chambers began. "He can write!"

At the words, Stubel began to rise with the same agility Dusty had noticed when he climbed out of the buggy. Being aware of the other's potential, Dusty did not dismiss him as a factor in the forthcoming events. Giving the plate before him a shove, Dusty sent it spinning across the table to fall and dump its contents into Stubel's lap. Although the stew had been out of the pan for some time, it retained sufficient warmth to be noticeable. Pure reflex reaction caused Stubel to jerk away from the glutinous mixture. In doing so, his legs became entangled with those of the chair which crumpled under his weight and dumped him on his well-padded rump.

On hearing Chambers' comment, Dobley

sprang from the table. He realized that he held a weapon more readily available even than his holstered revolver, so started to draw back the hammer of Calamity's Colt. Equally aware of that fact, Calamity snatched the skillet from the wall at the first hint of trouble. Lacking the time to raise it, she gripped its handle with both hands and swung sideways at waist level. Coming around, the edge of the skillet sliced into Dobley's belly with considerable force. With a strangled croak, the man doubled over. The Colt dropped from his fingers as both hands went instinctively to his pain-knotted belly. Stumbling rearwards, he turned and collapsed by the door.

"That'll teach you to fuss with Dusty Fog's lil wife!" Calamity yelled and turned her attention to the centre of the room.

Springing forward fast, Lip grabbed Dusty by the left upper arm, using both hands to haul him from his chair. Slightly slower, due to his surprise at learning their "victim" could read and write, Chambers advanced along the other side of the table to lend his companion a helping hand. Fortunately for Dusty, neither of his attackers thought to draw their guns.

Coming up faster than Lip tried to pull him, Dusty set about freeing his arm from the other's grip. The position of Lip's arms prevented Dusty from driving a blow into his body, so he wasted no time trying. Instead he brought his right arm around in a swinging arc and raked his stiff fingers across the other's eyes. Pain and protective instinct caused Lip to lean backwards and jerk his head away from the danger, although he did not release Dusty's arm. Not immediately anyway. Bending his right elbow at the end of its swing Dusty drove it down to crash into the centre of Lip's chest. Feeling as if a mule had kicked him, Lip lost his hold and stumbled away. He collided with the sidepiece hard enough to bounce the hat off the hidden Colt.

Free from Lip, Dusty prepared to handle Chambers. With his back to the hard-case, Dusty knew he could not turn in time to stop him. Twisting his torso slightly, so he could see the man, Dusty leaned forward away from his clutching hands. Raising the left leg, Dusty drove it behind him. Chambers took Dusty's foot in the pit of the stomach. When dressing for the deception, Dusty had retained his cowhand boots and chanced

222

them going unnoticed. Designed to spike into the earth and hold firm against the pull of a roped animal, these boots made mighty fine kicking tools; as Chambers might have profanely testified had he been able to mention the matter. Bringing down his foot, Dusty pivoted around and lashed a bare-hand slap to the side of the man's head. Spun around by the force of the blow, Chambers rushed in Calamity's direction. Never one to miss entering into the spirit of things, she swung around the skillet. Metal rang on bone as the bottom of the skillet met Chambers' head. Even without the girl's attentions, he would have been out of the fight for a spell. Calamity made sure he would not be in any shape to come back at all.

Showing a fair turn of speed, Stubel regained his feet and sent his right hand flashing to the short-barrelled Smith & Wesson holstered under his left arm. Calamity yelled a warning, dropping the skillet and bending to pick up her Colt. Already Dusty was springing forward, his left hand sweeping around to the outside of Stubel's right elbow. Pushing the arm to the left, he tried to block the draw. Stubel struggled against Dusty's push with enough strength to warn that other measures would be needed to disarm him.

Finding himself unable to hold the gun in its holster, Dusty slipped his right hand between Stubel's right arm and body to grip the wrist on the inside. With the grip secured, Dusty slid his left hand down to close on the trapped wrist from the other side. Although Stubel had managed to get the revolver free and from under his jacket, he could not turn the barrel in his captor's direction. Swiftly Dusty jerked the wrist down and to the rear, turning it against the joint of the elbow's natural bend as he continued to move it up again. Pain and a desire to avoid a dislocated arm caused Stubel to open his fingers. The Smith & Wesson fell from them as his feet left the floor. Sailing over, he landed on his back, bounced twice and came to a halt in a corner of the room.

About the same time Lip recovered sufficiently to become aware of the Colt lying close to his hand. Grabbing it up, he thrust himself around and away from the sidepiece.

"Dusty!" Calamity yelled as she scooped up her Colt and tossed it in his direction.

Even as Dusty's fingers closed around the ivory butt, he saw Lip lining his own Colt at him. Throwing himself aside, Dusty saw flame spark from the four and three quarter inch barrel and heard the slap of a close passing bullet. Then he landed on the floor facing the man and rolled on to his stomach. Holding an unfamiliar weapon, he did not dare try any fancy shooting. With the Colt's trigger held back by his right forefinger, he brought the heel of his left palm around to the hammer spur.

Stroking back the hammer, he released it and repeated the movement three more times. Fanning could not produce extreme accuracy even at close range, but it offered the fastest known method of turning lead loose from a single-action revolver.

And at that moment speed rather than bull's eye accuracy was what Dusty wanted. Four times in less than three seconds the Colt roared, throwing a cloud of swirling powder smoke in addition to its bullets. Several years had passed since Dusty had last handled a revolver of so light a calibre as the Navy Colt and the recoil kick did not even approach the wrist-jolting slam of a Peacemaker. So he could control the gun with greater ease and sent its bullets in a close pattern. Four holes leapt into the centre of Lip's chest while he was still cocking Dusty's Colt, slamming him back against the sidepiece. For a moment he hung there, his hand falling to his side and the Colt slipping to the floor. Then he flopped forward and down.

Raising himself into a sitting position. Stubel looked around in a dazed manner. At the sight of the bone-handled Peacemaker by the sidepiece, he tensed and prepared to dive towards it. The click of a cocking Colt came to his ears followed by a quiet, yet menacing warning in a Texas drawl.

"Leave it there, feller. You don't need it at all."

Slowly turning his eyes in the speaker's direction, Stubel found a transformation had come over the small, insignificant "victim". In some way he looked bigger, more powerful and commanding. There was a significance in the competent manner he held the Colt. There stood a *big* man.

"It appears to be the advisable thing to do," Stubel admitted and went on in an aggrieved tone, "Where the hell is Salty?"

"Likely he's got troubles of his own," Dusty guessed.

Which proved to be a shrewd assessment of the situation. Of course Dusty had the advantage of knowing of another unsuspected factor in the game.

After satisfying himself that the hiding place selected by Hudson could be relied on to do its work, the Ysabel Kid left the farm's owners to watch the horses. Picking his route carefully, he returned to the vicinity of the house. While the talking went on before the building, the Kid concealed himself behind the lean-to which sheltered the Hudsons' buckboard. Following Dusty's orders, he waited ready to throw the weight of his magnificent Winchester in should it be required.

Hearing the commotion inside the cabin, Salty concluded he might be needed. So, drawing his revolver, he started towards the door unaware that the noise had attracted another person's attention.

"Let's you and me stay out here a spell, *hombre*," suggested the Kid, stepping from behind the lean-to.

Skidding into a turning halt, Salty tried to line his revolver on the speaker, a foolish action as the Kid's deadly Winchester was nestled in position against his shoulder and he was looking along its sights. Seeing Salty intended to fight, the Kid obliged him.

However, recalling Dusty's insistence on living prisoners who could be induced to talk, he pointed the rifle with care. A touch of the lightly adjusted set-trigger sent a bullet which ploughed through Salty's leg, tumbling him in a yelping heap to the ground.

At the same moment guns roared in the cabin, their sounds merging with the Winchester's bark. First a Peacemaker, then the rapid cracking of a lighter gun. Anxiety bit at the Kid. While Calamity could handle her Navy Colt with some skill, he doubted if she could get off shots that fast from it. Which could mean Dusty needed help in the worst kind of way.

Bounding forward, he raced towards the cabin's door. In passing he kicked Salty's gun away from the man's side. Nor did fears for his friends' safety cause him to forget the basic precautions. No more shots came from inside, but that proved nothing. If Dusty was in command of the situation, he must be told a friend was entering the room. Should the small Texan be down—the Kid tried not to think of that. Instead he let out a *Pehnane* war whoop, kicked open the door and went through it fast. Halting, his rifle made an arc around the cabin and he took in the sights. It seemed that his fears had been groundless, for Dusty was in full control.

"What're you trying to do?" Calamity demanded, glaring indignantly at the new arrival. "Deafen us. And take your hat off in my kitchen."

Seeing that both his friends had suffered no damage in the fighting, the Kid relaxed. Cradling his rifle on the crook of the left arm, he eyed the girl up and down for a moment.

"Calam, honey," he said. "You sure look elegant and fetching in that there dress."

"One more funny out of you, Lon Ysabel!" she yelled, reaching for the skillet, "and I'm going to raise lumps all over your Injun head."

"My ole pappy allus used to tell me never to sass a woman in her own kitchen," grinned the Kid. "See you got 'em, Dusty."

"How about the one outside?" Dusty asked.

"Won't be walking for a spell, but he's alive like you wanted."

"It seems that I have been a victim of trickery and skulduggery," Stubel remarked. "From what I heard, you are Dusty Fog, sir?"

"You've never been righter," Calamity told him.

An expression of near relief flickered across the chubby features. "I'm pleased to know I heard a-right. The mortification would be too great if I'd been outwitted by some country bumpkin or Pinkerton sneak."

"Yeah," said the practical Miss Canary. "If you're so happied up about it, you can help me clean up the mess you've made."

After the cleaning up had been performed to Calamity's satisfaction, the body removed, wounds tended to and the prisoners secured, Stubel sat with Dusty, Calamity and the Kid.

"May I ask how you came to be on my trail?" he inquired.

"The Wilsons met Calamity on the way to Mulrooney—" Dusty began.

"Only I smelled a tricky fat rat and took 'em to see Cap'n Dusty at Trail End," Calamity interrupted.

"Your animosity is justified, young lady," Stubel told her in a pained voice. "But, please, not 'fat'. I prefer the term 'well-padded'."

"Have it your way," Calamity grinned. "You're a cool one, I'll give you that!"

"Cool, maybe. But hardly as smart as I

believed. Of course, Captain Fog, it was pure good fortune which led you to the right place at the right time."

"Not all the way," Dusty objected. "We arrested two of your men in Trail End and learned about the other places you'd bought. Working from them, it wasn't hard to figure you were headed west along the Deccan Valley. Got the map, picked these farms and made for them. The rest was easy."

"May I congratulate you on your performance?" Stubel asked. "Possibly a little overdone in retrospect, but adequate, sir, most adequate." He gave a low sigh. "And anyway, if I may say so without causing offence, one finds it difficult to reconcile your appearance with your reputation."

"What the hell's that mean?" demanded Calamity.

"That one might expect Captain Fog to be a man of greater, more imposing stature, my dear," Stubel explained. "He does, if he will pardon me saying it, lack height."

"You know something?" Calamity said soberly. "I never noticed that."

Part Three

MONDAY IS A QUIET DAY

"YOU'VE sure got to hand it to the Yankee Army," Mark Counter growled after reading the letter handed to him by Dusty Fog. "Damned if they don't want us to take their deserters back as well as catching them."

After turning over the land-swindlers to the county sheriff and seeing Calamity Jane depart about her own business, the Texans had continued the work of cleaning up Trail End. In addition to combating the efforts of the dishonest element among the town's residents, Dusty and his deputies found other peace officer work demanded their attention.

On Friday morning, a week after Dusty's return from the Deccan Valley, a professional informer called Mousey arrived with news. He claimed that four deserters from the United States Army were in town, celebrating the theft of a shipment of Springfield carbines on its way to Fort Debdale.

Descending on the hog-ranch where the quartet were relaxing after a night of debauchery, the Texans captured them without fuss or bloodshed. When he sent a telegraph message to the Fort, informing its commanding officer of the capture, Dusty thought he need only hold the men in jail until a military escort arrived to collect them. Instead a soldier brought a letter from the colonel in command, asking that the town's deputies deliver the deserters to the Fort. A full-scale review and inspection by top brass from Washington called for the presence of all personnel, preventing the Fort from providing its own collection party. However the colonel felt an early start should be made at interrogating the quartet about the theft of the carbines and hoped Dusty could oblige him.

While Dusty appreciated the colonel's difficulties, he wished that some other arrangements had been made to take the men off his hands. With four such desperate men in the jail, Dusty had insisted on two deputies remaining at the office instead of the one who could handle the usual run of drunks and minor offenders which mostly occupied the cells. That had meant handling the town on

Friday and Saturday with only two men at his back. Only by constant patrolling did they hold the celebrating visitors under control and prevent complaints from the City Fathers. Dusty did not wish to continue working under such a handicap.

"What'll we do then?" Waco inquired.

"We'll have to send them back like he asks," Dusty replied. "I can't keep two of you tied down in the office and the sooner we get rid of them the better."

"Who'll be going?" Mark wanted to know.

"You, Lon and Waco."

"Three of us?" the Kid put in.

"There's four of them," Dusty pointed out. "And Mousey was back last night to say he'd heard the feller they sold the carbines to figured to get them free."

"That means the boy and me guarding them," Mark told the Kid. "And you riding circle to make sure nobody sneaks up and takes them away from us."

"Fear not!" declared the Kid, striking a pose much favoured by dramatic actors of the day. "I'll protect you."

"*That*'s what we're fearing," grinned Waco. "Anyways, if there is a try to get 'em loose, it'd be better happening out of town."

"Yeah," agreed Doc. "Happen another bunch tried it, folks might start to reckon we don't make our prisoners comfortable in jail. A thing like that could ruin us socially."

"When do we start?" Mark asked.

"Tomorrow, just afore sun-up," Dusty replied. "No sense in letting too many folks know you've gone. All goes well, you should be back here by noon Tuesday."

"Easy enough," Mark said. "Reckon you and Doc can handle things here?"

"I reckon we can. There's no fresh trail drive expected until Wednesday at the soonest and you'll be back by then. Monday's a quiet day, so we should be all right."

"Life'll likely be more peaceful with you three gone," Doc went on after Dusty had finished his views on the matter. "You fixing to tell Mayor Galt about sending the boys off, Dusty?"

"If he asks about 'em," Dusty answered. "Given just a mite of luck, he'll never know they've gone."

Despite the care exercised by the floating outfit, the departure had one witness. In fact Wally Wade had spent the night hiding in an empty shack behind the jail watching for it.

From his place, he saw the sullen-faced prisoners led out, mounted on the waiting horses and secured in the saddles.

"Don't you pair work yourselves too hard while we're gone," Wade heard Waco say as he, Mark Counter and the Ysabel Kid swung into their saddles.

"Not them," the Kid went on. "They'll be sat back nice and easy while we do all the work."

"The Good Lord knows who deserves the most," grinned Doc Leroy. "Don't make too much noise riding off, I'm going back to bed."

"Don't know why you troubled to get up," Mark told him. "Let's go. Take a point, Lon."

Wade watched the Kid ride off into the grey light of the dawn, followed by his two companions and the prisoners. Waiting until Dusty and Doc had returned inside the jail, Wade rose and backed away from the window. He grunted a little at the stiffness of his legs, then a grin crossed his unshaven face.

"Damned if ole Chesil didn't pull it off," he thought. "I'd best go tell him that three of 'em's gone."

Leaving the shack, he slouched off in the

direction of the livery barn. Only at the moment of exit did he show any caution. Once clear of the building, he walked along openly. A tall, lean, sun-bronzed man in worn range clothes, he looked little different from the usual run of trail hand who came north with the Texas cattle. Certainly the Negro at the barn saw nothing suspicious nor alarming in his appearance and arrival at that early hour.

"That was some night I've had," Wade remarked as he collected his horse and saddle. "This town's all I've heard it was."

"Yes, sah," replied the Negro disinterestedly and Wade realized that he need not bother going further in explanation of his pre-dawn departure. All the stable hand wanted to do was see him go and return to an interrupted sleep.

Nobody showed any interest in the sight of Wade riding out of town. However, once clear he set his horse moving at a fast pace and avoided human habitation as he headed west. At last, after keeping clear of the occasional farm, he rode towards a good-sized cabin sheltered on the banks of a stream in a valley.

A chance onlooker, knowing Wade's purpose to be dishonest, might have felt puzzled at his making for such a prosperous, respectable looking place. That was the chief charm of Gus Tibor's farm as a hideout for the select few outlaws who knew of it. Other places often advertised their main source of income by the owner's prosperity clashing with the decrepit, neglected state of the property. Not so Tibor. He ran his farm efficiently and never spent money in excess to what he could have earned legitimately. While he charged a high price for his services, those who used them regarded the money well spent.

Leaving his horse in the barn, Wade went to the house and entered the kitchen. Seated around the table, the other members of his gang greeted him and waited eagerly to hear his news. They looked like a cross-section of trail end town visitors. Tall, elegantly dressed in the cutaway coat, fancy vest and frilly fronted shirt of a professional gambler, Hiram Chesil had a handsome face that, graced with long moustachios, once won him acclaim as a villain in the theatre. However the pearl-handled Colt in the contoured holster at his right side was no mere actor's prop. Herb Snell and Pip Russon looked like a couple of brawny gandy-dancers from a railroad construction crew. Short, stocky, bearded Seth Turner might have been a freight wagon driver, with his buckskin jacket and pants tucked into heavy, low heeled boots and a bull whip thrust into the waist band. Last of the party, Jackie White was a typical trail end town loafer. Tall, lean, young, he wore cowhand dress and might have passed as one to untutored eyes. Having lost his gunbelt and revolver in a poker game before being invited to join the gang, he carried a battered 1860 Army Colt in his waistband.

"It worked," Wade announced. "Fog sent Counter, the Kid and that young un off with the deserters."

"Just as I expected," Chesil replied. "I thought he would send three of them at least when he heard that whisper I started about a rescue attempt."

"When do we take the bank?" Jackie demanded eagerly.

Chesil studied the young man in a pained manner. Only sheer necessity had caused the one-time actor to take Jackie into his confidence. However the young man's part in the affair called for no great exercise of mentality. He would hold the horses for the other members of the gang and act as lookout while they did their work. It seemed from his question that Jackie had forgotten everything Chesil had told him about the conduct of the robbery.

"Tonight, as we planned," Chesil answered. "And not until after we've made sure that Fog and Leroy can't interfere."

"What if we don't get them?" Turner inquired.

"We leave it!" Chesil stated. "That's the way we planned it from the start. Let me tell you again. First, the bank's manager works late every Monday. He'll be leaving at around half after nine. We can grab him as he leaves, go back in, empty the safe and be out of Trail End before ten—as long as Fog and Leroy aren't around."

"We could take them—" Jackie began.

"There're dead men from here to Texas who thought that," Chesil interrupted. "Since they took over, Fog has had two of his men around each Monday to see the banker gets away safely. I don't want them there when we make our move."

"And you reckon we can get them?" Russon growled. "How d'you know they'll be making the rounds separate instead of together?"

"I admit it's guess work," Chesil replied.

"But it's a better than fair chance. Fog won't want it known he's sent three men out, so he and Leroy'll circulate and show themselves regularly around town. It's Monday and should be a quiet night, so they'll work separately instead of going around together."

"You want them taken alive?" Snell said doubtfully.

"If we can. Without shooting or too much noise anyway. Don't forget, the penalty for killing a peace officer is a whole heap more severe and permanent than for robbing a bank."

"Kill Fog or Leroy and you'll never know another safe day as long as you live," Wade warned. "Every friend they've got won't rest until they've nailed our hides to the wall. And they've got friends I don't want hunting me."

"Or me," Turner breathed fervently. "I was working for Lanton down to Azul Rio and know. Fog passed the word and King Fisher, Ben 'n' Billy Thompson, Wes Hardin and damned near every top gun in Texas come running to help him."

"Just remember that!" Chesil went on grimly. "I, for one, want to use my share of the loot on good living; not have to spend it hiding out. All right, it's time to get moving.

You and Pip go first, Herb. Leave your horses in that hollow I showed you and walk into town, we'll bring them with us when we come. Stick around the railroaders' places until it's time to meet me—and stay sober."

"Sure," Snell replied, feeling a little rankled at Chesil's repetition of the warning. Anyone would think that the fancy-talking tinhorn alone had experience as an outlaw, or the ability to do some smart figuring. "Let's go, Pip."

"Walt, you stay clear of all of us until sun down. Then meet Seth as if by accident. I'm counting on you two to take Dusty Fog out of the game."

"We'll do it," Wade promised. "His office's the last place he'll expect to find trouble."

"Fog'll be the biggest danger," Chesil emphasized. "When we've got him, we'll go after Leroy."

"How about me?" Jackie asked.

"You'll be with me," Chesil told him. "The manager at Stoeger's thinks I'm going to run a private poker game in my room and he'll take you for my steerer."

Any objections Jackie felt at being assigned such a minor role died unsaid. Looking around, he saw that the other members of the gang whole-heartedly approved of Chesil's decision. Annoyance nagged at him, but he kept it under control. The time would come, he felt sure, when he could prove his worth and make the rest of the bunch eat crow.

Studying the young man, Chesil felt a resurgence of his misgivings. Wade, Turner, Snell and Russon were all experienced outlaws with reputations for reliability if not brilliance. Such men could be relied upon to keep their heads and follow orders. To Chesil's mind, Jackie formed the weak link in the chain. However time and circumstances did not permit them to look for a more capable replacement.

"We'll be going," Snell said, standing up and turning from the table.

"Don't forget," Chesil replied. "Do what I told you and make sure you keep sober."

If Chesil had seen the angry scowl which twisted Snell's face, he might have regretted repeating the often-made warning on the matter of sobriety. However he was too full of his thoughts on how well the affair was progressing to realize that his air of superiority had riled at least one member of the gang.

"Town's quiet enough so far," Dusty remarked, watching Doc Leroy light the office's lamp.

"It mostly is on Monday," the slim cowhand replied and hung the lamp in its place above the desk. "Let's hope it stays that way."

"I wish we'd a jailer," Dusty remarked. "Way we are, I've either got to leave one of you boys here, or have the office empty while we make the rounds."

"Galt allows the town can't afford any more law," Doc said. "I've filled all the lamps. We don't want them going out on us."

"That's for sure. I reckon we'd best start showing the folks their lawmen's doing the job."

"There's nothing like contented tax-payers," Doc grinned. "I reckon I'll drift down to the railroad depot and watch the train come in."

"Then I'll stick on the other side of town," Dusty decided. "If you need help, shout for it."

"Count on me for that," Doc answered and walked from the office.

Doc's visit to the railroad depot went by uneventfully. No undesirable characters were travelling on the train to demand his attention and it pulled out leaving Trail End at least no worse than when it arrived. After a moment's thought and a study of the quiet streets, Doc directed his feet towards Annie Gash's hog-ranch. Not that he expected to find any trouble there, but felt a visit would be worthwhile. In addition to running the plushiest and most honest brothel in town, Annie served up delicious turkey sandwiches and the best cup of coffee Doc had tasted since the Wedge disbanded. More than that, she could be relied upon to produce both should a hard-working peace officer call in.

"There's some'd call it bribery and corruption," Doc mused. "But I allow it's appreciation for devotion to duty."

With his conscience salved, Doc visited the brothel and enjoyed a meal. Hunger staved off, he headed towards the busier part of town. His route took him towards the rear of Stoeger's hotel and by a deserted but open blacksmith's shop. Pausing long enough to discover that the owner had merely left the shop to quench his thirst at a saloon, he walked on towards the hotel.

A low groan came to Doc's ears and drew his eyes to the corner of the building. Leaning against it and sagging down, a man let out another moan of pain. Instantly Doc's leisurely attitude changed and he strode forward fast. Seeing another human being apparently in pain, his instincts as a doctor over-rode those of the peace officer. No matter how he came to be in such distress, the man sounded like he needed medical attention and Doc went to give it to him.

Despite Chesil's warnings, or maybe because of them, Herb Snell drank just a little more whiskey than was safe. While not sufficient to make him openly indiscreet, the raw liquor's bite increased animosity against his leader.

"Damned tinhorn!" Snell muttered as he and Russon approached the rear of Stoeger's Hotel. "Does he reckon he's the only smart cuss in the world?"

"Acts like it," Russon admitted.

"Well he ain't!" Snell snorted. "I've worked with—Down the alley, quick!"

That had been their intention in the first place, so Russon wondered what caused the other man's hurried command. Before he could ask, Snell caught him by the arm and jerked him into the darkness of the alley.

"What's up?" Russon hissed.

"Look out there," Snell replied, peering

cautiously around the corner. "By the blacksmith's shop. Don't show yourself."

Impressed by the other's excitement, Russon obeyed. He saw a tall, slim Texan standing before the blacksmith's shop and reading a notice fastened to its open door. Even before the Texan turned and the shop's lights glinted on a badge pinned to his jacket, Russon recognized him.

"That's Doc Leroy!"

"I figured he was too small to be Dusty Fog," Snell sniffed.

"What'll we do?" Russon whispered as they drew back behind the shelter of the corner.

"Take him. What else?"

"Chesil said we should see him afore we made a move."

If anything, the reminder hardened Snell's intention to act. Sure Chesil had produced the plan, but that did not stop a man making the most of any chance which came his way. Likely they would not find a better opportunity to grab off Doc Leroy than at that moment.

"Go out there and make like you're hurting bad. You know how to do it better 'n' me,"

Snell hissed. "Get him over here and I'll do the rest."

Although not sure whether they were doing the right thing, Russon obeyed. Staggering around the corner, he gave a stirring impersonation of a hurt or sick man. The sight and sound of Russon's act brought Doc Leroy towards him, just as Snell had anticipated it would. Gun in hand, Snell waited behind the wall. Despite the vague stirrings of doubt that crept into his head, he prepared to carry out his improvement to Chesil's scheme.

"What's up, mister?" Doc asked, bending over the crouching shape.

Just an instant too late he realized the danger. A soft foot fall came to his ears and he tried to straighten up, right hand flashing towards its Colt. Russon grabbed hold of Doc's lapels, holding him down for the vital moment Snell needed to take a hand. Coming around the corner, Snell swung his revolver's barrel at Doc's head. While the hat took the worst force of the blow, it still landed hard enough to collapse Doc unconscious across Russon's crouching frame.

"Got him!" Snell enthused, standing ready to deliver another blow.

"What'll we do with him?" Russon demanded, rolling the limp body from him and standing up. "We can't just leave him here or in the alley, somebody might find him."

That same question had formed the basis of Snell's doubts as he launched his attack. Being so eager to put one over on Chesil, he had blindly ignored the most important aspect of the capture. The buildings all around showed signs of occupation and could not be used. Nor could they chance standing around discussing alternative arrangements in case the blacksmith returned and saw them.

"Go see if there's anybody in the back of the hotel," Snell ordered. "If the way's clear, we'll take him up to Chesil's room. It's number twelve, upstairs at the front."

Having no alternative plan available, Russon raised no objections. Hurrying to the building's rear entrance, he opened it and looked inside.

"It's clear," he said with relief. "Let's move."

"What the hell—!" Chesil gasped, opening the door of his room at Snell's knock and staring at the limp shape hung between the two men. "Get in here, fast!"

"We got Leroy," Snell announced unnecessarily as they entered with their burden.

"So I see!" Chesil growled. "Did anybody see you bringing him up here?"

"Naw," Snell scoffed. "We come up the back way, real careful. Get him on the bed, Pip."

Chesil closed and locked the door while the two men carried Doc over and laid him on the bed. Anger flushed the handsome features as Chesil swung to face his helpers.

"Why in hell did you do it?"

"Seemed like a good idea at the time," Russon answered.

"We saw Leroy coming, with nobody around, so we figured to take our chance and grab him," Snell went on. "Get that fire rope off the chair, Jackie, so's we can hawg-tie him afore he wakes up."

"Sure, Herb," Jackie replied, crossing the room to where a length of rope lay on a chair. Like many Western hotels, Stoeiger's offered only primitive means of escape in case of a fire.

"We'd best get his gunbelt off as well," Snell continued and looked coldly at his leader. "You said you wanted Leroy and Fog. Well, here's one of 'em."

Chesil read a challenge in the words but decided to ignore it. At an earlier stage in the arrangements he could have dealt with such opposition, but not with the time for the robbery so close.

"All right," he said. "Gag and blindfold him. We'll go ahead as planned."

"Figured we might," Snell grinned, passing Doc's gunbelt to Jackie and taking the rope.

Drawing back from the bed, Jackie stared in awe almost at the belt. It surpassed any other gun-rig he had ever handled, both in design and craftsmanship. Whoever had tooled the leather knew his work. The holster flowed from the belt in a way which would hold it firm and present the Colt's butt most easily to the wearer's hand. Carefully shaped, it retained the gun perfectly, being neither too tight nor over loose. Such a holster would permit the kind of speed Jackie felt himself capable of producing given the chance. So would the ivory-handled Colt in the holster. Even without handling it, Jackie sensed that its mechanism had been smoothed and improved for greater ease of use. If he owned

251

such a gun and rig, he would never again be forced to accept a minor role—and share of the loot—in a robbery.

"Jackie!" Chesil said over his shoulder. "Go to the Golden Nugget and see if Wade or Turner's there. Get them up here as fast as you can."

"Sure," the youngster replied.

None of the other three looked his way, being absorbed in the business of securing their prisoner. For a moment he hesitated, then shrugged. All his companions owned a gunbelt, so why should he be less well equipped? With that thought in mind, he turned and crossed the room. Hardly daring to breathe in case he drew attention to himself and his plunder, he unlocked the door. Nobody spoke to him, so he stepped from the room still carrying the belt.

Once outside, with the door closed, he grinned broadly. The passage was deserted, so he stood strapping on the belt. No matter how he adjusted the buckle, he could not make the rig hang with complete comfort. Deciding that he could easily have the necessary alterations made at a later date, he fastened the pigging thongs around his leg. Then he swaggered downstairs and out of the hotel, trying to convey his wild, woolly and uncurried nature to all who saw him. Wearing a top-hand's gunbelt, he felt sure that he would soon prove his worth to the rest of the gang.

The fact that he had not seen Doc Leroy for some time caused Dusty no concern. An experienced peace officer, Doc knew the importance of being seen in the right places and the value of caution. If Doc should run into any serious trouble, he would try to let Dusty know of it before becoming involved.

As part of his patrol, Dusty walked by the Farmer's Bank and saw its manager working at the well-lit desk inside. There would be time to visit some of the saloons and make his presence felt before returning to watch over the man as he left and secured the bank for the night.

One of the places Dusty visited was the Golden Nugget. Run by an honest man, Dusty knew it to be one place in which he could relax for a time. Coming over, the owner greeted Dusty and offered to set up the drinks.

"Just a beer, Ras," Dusty replied,

accompanying the man to the bar. "It sure is peaceful tonight."

"Makes a change," O'Hagen, the owner, answered. "I can't complain, business could be worse. Anyways, with three of your boys out of town, you'll likely want it peaceful."

"I'd settle for it that way even with them here," Dusty said as a bartender slid a schooner of beer along to halt before him.

"This town's a whole heap better than it was afore you came," O'Hagen stated. "There's few who'd question that."

"I can't see everybody agreeing with you," Dusty grinned.

While talking, Dusty became aware of an uneasy feeling that somebody was looking at him. Any man who lived in danger as much as Dusty developed an instinct for the difference between a casual glance and intense observation. Alert for danger, Dusty set down his beer glass and made a leisurely-seeming, but thorough study of his surroundings. His eyes ran quickly over the customers, discounting O'Hagen's employees as the cause of his uneasiness. None of the local men showed interest in him, nor any of the groups of cowhands around the room.

That only left one man. Standing with his

left elbow on the bar top and right thumb hooked into his gunbelt close to the holstered Colt it carried, the man in question turned his head and stared too obviously away as Dusty's eyes swung in his direction.

In passing Dusty gave Jackie a complete scrutiny and summed up his character. Tall, gangling, a trail end bum trying to impress folks with his salty toughness was Dusty's correct, if unflattering, conclusion. Yet such a man could be dangerous, especially when he wore a fast-draw gun-rig. He looked on the prod and might wish to build a reputation by facing Dusty Fog. As soon as Dusty seemed to be looking elsewhere, the lean jasper's eyes swivelled back in his direction.

Unlike Jackie, Dusty knew how to keep unobserved watch on a person. So, while apparently absorbed in drinking his beer and talking with O'Hagen, the small Texan gave the gangling youngster a closer study. Despite its poor fit, the workmanship of the gunbelt was excellent. It was also a familiar style that Dusty recognized. Except that old Joe Gaylin, the El Paso leatherworker, would never make a belt for a trail end town bum.

Then Dusty tensed slightly and his fingers tightened on the beer schooner. Even along the length of the bar he could make out details of the belt, and in particular its buckle. The floral scroll work on the surface and rope effect around its edge might have been duplicated many times, but the letters M.E.L. in its centre told a grim story. Marvin Eldridge Leroy, the initials stood for; but Doc Leroy was not wearing the belt.

Keeping his face expressionless, Dusty finished the drink and set the glass on the bar. "Reckon I'd best get moving, Ras," he said.

"I should think so, for shame," the saloonkeeper grinned. "As a tax payer I expect the local law to be on the rounds twenty-*six* hours a day."

"You should let your taxes lapse," Dusty told him. "Don't take any wooden nickels."

With that Dusty walked across the room and out of the batwing doors. Not by a flicker did he show the concern he felt for Doc's safety. However, as he walked along in front of the saloon he darted a glance through its window. Just as he hoped the skinny young cuss sank the remains of his drink and headed for the door.

On his arrival at the Golden Nugget, Jackie saw nothing of the men he had come to collect. Knowing they were supposed to meet there, he leaned against the bar and awaited their arrival. After a short time he saw Dusty enter and could hardly believe his eyes.

Could that short-grown runt be the famous Dusty Fog?

Unlikely as it seemed, the newcomer wore the badge of town marshal and O'Hagen greeted him with genuine deference. Jackie felt cheated. Surely a man of Dusty Fog's reputation ought to be a veritable giant, eye-catching in every way.

"If that's the famous Dusty Fog, I could lick him one-handed," Jackie decided silently. "Left-handed at that."

And so an idea began to form. What if he, Jackie, the despised underling took on to handle the menial work, brought in Dusty Fog? That would change the others' attitude towards him. Taking Dusty Fog would be so easy too. Clearly he did not suspect anything might be wrong in his town. When he left, Jackie could follow and grab him in some dark alley. Dealing with that runt would be simple as long as he did not have a chance to go for his guns. A quick rush, the swing of a fist or the Colt's barrel, and it would be all over bar delivering his prisoner to Chesil and demanding a bigger cut of the loot.

Filled with such pleasant visions, Jackie watched Dusty leave the saloon. As he finished his drink, the youngster saw his victim turn to the left and stroll off along the sidewalk. Only with an effort did Jackie control himself, fighting down a desire to hurry, and amble in a casual manner from the room. Outside, he looked along the street. A low growl of annoyance broke from him, for the small Texan was not in sight. Of course a dark area lay beyond the end of the saloon, its neighbouring building being closed for the night. Fog would be walking through the darkness, not all that far ahead.

Eagerly Jackie started forward. Ahead of him the sidewalk ended at the corner of the saloon, leaving a gap through which wagons could deliver supplies to the rear entrance. Eyes fixed on the front of the next building, Jackie reached the end of the Golden Nugget and dropped from the boards to the ground.

A hand came from the blackness of the alley, laying hold of his vest and heaving at it with savage strength. With a startled yelp, the lean youngster felt himself swung from the street, around in a half circle and smashed face-first into the saloon's wall. Dazed by the unexpected attack, he could not resist being turned around again. In desperation he tried to claw the Colt from its holster. A hard fist ripped into the pit of his stomach, knifing torment through him and causing him to clutch at the stricken area instead of the gun's ivory butt. Nor could he double up to lessen the pain. Coming up under his chin, an arm which felt as hard as steel laid itself across his throat and pinned him against the wall. Croaking in pain and terror, he felt the Colt jerked from its holster. He heard its hammer click back, then felt the cold touch of its muzzle against his nose.

"Where'd you get Doc Leroy's belt and gun?" demanded a cold, savage voice and the pressure on his throat relaxed just enough to allow him to answer.

"I—I dun—!"

"Don't fuss me, boy!" the voice cut in as the arm thrust home to chop off his lie. The Colt moved from his nose, but the barrel tapped against its bridge hard enough to be felt. "Where is he?"

"M—My gang's got him!" Jackie croaked as the arm moved away slightly.

"*Your* gang?" Dusty repeated, the word of contempt in his voice.

"S—So help me, it's true! They grabbed him as a hostage—"

"Is he hurt?"

"No!" Jackie almost screamed the word out, feeling certain any other answer would bring painful repercussions. "We just grabbed him as a hostage."

"For what?"

"Th—Them four deserters. You've got to turn 'em loose and we'll let Leroy go in exchange."

"Where're they holding him?" Dusty asked. "If you want a face comes morning you'd best answer up *pronto*."

"O—Outside town," Jackie lied, speaking fast in the hope that it did not show. "In a draw close to the railroad track, maybe a mile to the west."

Given any amount of luck the gang might still save him, Jackie figured. If so, he wanted to be able to claim that he had not disclosed their true plans. It seemed that Dusty Fog accepted the story. His arm moved from Jackie's throat, took hold of the youngster's right shoulder and turned him to face the wall once more. After a brief pause Jackie felt his right arm seized and drawn behind him. Something cold and steely clicked about the wrist, squeezing with a somehow frightening pressure on the bones. Before Jackie could realize that to handcuff him Dusty Fog must have put the Colt into his waistband, the left wrist was taken back and secured to the right.

"Start walking," Dusty ordered, stepping clear.

"Where to?" Jackie whined.

"Jail, where else?" Dusty replied. "You figure I'm asking you to be my partner at a box-social?"

With that he shoved the youngster ahead of him into the street. A couple of townsmen about to enter the Golden Nugget halted and watched Dusty heading Jackie towards the jail, then went through the batwing doors.

Following Jackie, Dusty stayed alert. He did not know if the youngster had spoken the truth about the reason for Doc's capture but left a more searching inquiry until they reached the office. Once in a cell and given suitable inducements, Dusty felt the scared young man would tell him all he needed to know.

The section of street which housed the jail and marshal's office was deserted as Dusty brought his prisoner along it. Nor could he see any sign of life in the buildings on either side. All of them, including Dusty's office, lay silent and in darkness.

"Damn it, Jackie's taking his own good time!" Snell growled, stalking across the hotel room to the window, then back to the table.

"Maybe Wade and Turner haven't showed at the Golden Nugget," Chesil replied. "Stop tramping around like that. There're folk in the room below and we don't want them complaining to the manager."

"I thought you'd squared him," Snell sniffed.

"Only to run a private poker game, not a square dance."

Sensing trouble between his two colleagues, Russon decided to take their attention from each other.

"What'll we do about him?" he asked, indicating the bound, gagged and blindfolded shape of Leroy on the bed.

"Leave him when we go. He can't recognize any of us and it'll be morning at the earliest before anybody finds him," Chesil replied, glancing around the room. Then he stiffened and snarled. "Where's Leroy's gunbelt?"

"I give it to Jac—" Snell began.

"And he's took it out with him!" Russon went on. "That stupid kid!" He's likely to think a rig like that makes him as fast as Dusty Fog."

"Come on!" Chesil barked. "We'd best get after him. And we'll have to start hunting for Fog with or without Wade and Turner soon, or it'll be too late."

"You leaving your saddlebags here?" Snell inquired.

"Yes. I don't want to carry them round with me. I'll collect them before we go to pull the raid."

Doc listened to the feet thud across the room, the door open and close, then the key click in the lock. For a moment he lay still, ears straining to catch a sound to tell him if one of the gang remained in the room. After a few seconds he knew he was alone. There would be no point in leaving a guard, not in such a manner, for he could not escape. Tugging at the ropes about his arms and wrists told him that, as did the feel of the knots. Whoever had tied him knew more than a little about the game. Escaping from the bonds without aid would be practically impossible.

Which meant that he must somehow get aid. The problem being how to do it.

Then Doc remembered Chesil's warning about disturbing the people below. That could be the answer. Bracing himself, he bounced his rump into the air and down on the bed. After half-a-dozen attempts, he decided the noise made in such a manner would be inconsiderable. Setting his teeth, he swung his bound legs off the bed and lurched into a sitting position. Slowly he raised his bent knees and slammed his feet on to the floor. Being experienced in Western hotels, he could imagine what kind of racket his high-heeled cowhand boots made on the floorboards. Everything depended on the occupant of the room below being in it and whether his complaints had sufficient weight to over-ride the manager's bribe-bought loyalty to the outlaws.

Sitting on the bed, Doc found that he had set himself a hard task. The ropes binding tightened cruelly due to the change of position. With his mouth firmly blocked by the gag, he could not use it as an aid to breathing. Sweat poured from him, burning into his eyes beneath the blindfold and he could do nothing to prevent it. For all that, he refused to give up his only slender chance of escape. Gritting his teeth on the gag, he forced himself to continue stamping as hard as he could.

To give Wade and Turner full credit, they had arrived in Trail End with the intention of carrying out Chesil's orders all the way. However they found time dragging heavily and even since the start of the big clean up, the town offered numerous pleasures to divert bored visitors.

A compulsive gambler, Turner possessed a system calculated to ensure consistent winnings. That it regularly failed to produce the desired result did little to shake his faith, for he knew a number of ways to excuse its failure. Of course, the system would pick that of all days to come into its own. While visiting Eggars' saloon for a beer, he decided to buck the tiger a couple of whirls. The cards dictated by his system won—luck and the fact that Eggars' faro games now operated honestly probably helped—so he stayed on, oblivious of the clock's fingers turning closer to the hour when he must help rob the Farmers Bank.

Not that Wade was entirely blameless,

although his taste ran more to the pleasures of the flesh. Visiting the establishment of Annie Gash's chief rival, he selected company for a brief dalliance. The girl proved to be so charming and accomplished at her work, that he stayed on for far longer than he originally intended.

Before either man realized it, he had gone by the time when he should be at Stoeger's Hotel and receiving his final instructions. Taking as hurried a departure as possible from their pleasures, they met on the main street instead of at the Golden Nugget.

"Chesil's not going to like this," Wade warned.

"That don't throw me," Turner replied, having taken a few drinks to celebrate his system's success. Not enough to impair his efficiency, but sufficient to put a truculent edge on his temper. "Let's go see him."

Not wishing to argue, Wade nodded and they turned in the direction of the hotel. They walked along the street and passed in front of the marshal's office.

"Neither of 'em's in," Wade remarked, glancing through the window.

"Figures," Turner replied. "With the other three out of town, Fog and Leroy'll be on the streets. They don't have a jailer."

"Like Chesil said, they'll be coming back regular to see everything's all right," Wade commented thoughtfully. "Trouble being, time we've seen him and got back here, they're likely to have come and gone."

"Let's wait for them now," Turner suggested.

"I dunno," Wade replied hesitantly. "Chesil said we should see him—"

"Chesil ain't the only one's c'n think," Turner growled. "If we don't get Fog and Leroy, we don't get the bank. So let's grab us our chance while we can."

"There's nobody around," Wade admitted, darting a glance along the street.

"That's another thing. We might not be so lucky if we leave it," Turner pointed out. "Can't do any harm to wait a spell, anyways. If we ain't nailed at least one of 'em in half an hour, we'll go meet Chesil."

For a moment Wade hesitated, then he nodded his agreement. "Just for half an hour then."

That would still give them the bare minimum of time to bring off the robbery. If Chesil and the rest of the gang had already dealt with the lawmen, nothing would be lost.

Should Fog, Leroy, or both, return, they would be unlikely to expect danger in their office and so would fall into the waiting pair's hands. If that happened, the raid could take place as planned.

Entering the office, they paused and listened in case the cells should be occupied. No sound came, so Wade crossed to the desk and pointed to the lamp over it.

"Best put this out," he said. "They'll think it ran out of oil."

"Sure," Turner agreed. "Then we'll wait by the door and I'll whomp 'em over the head with the handle of this whip as they come in."

Standing one on each side of the front door, the men waited tense and expectant. Outside the street lay dark and silent, almost as if the citizens and visitors were combining to help Chesil's plan work. Neither Wade nor Turner felt completely at ease and grew less so by the minute. All too well they knew the nature of the men they were stalking. Let there be only a split-second's delay in handling Dusty Fog or Doc Leroy and at least one of the attackers stood a better than even chance of winding up with a bullet in him.

So the sound of approaching footsteps filled

them with mingled emotions. Silently Wade moved to the window and peered out. No longer did he regard the darkness of the street as a blessing, for it prevented him from seeing more than a blurred human shape passing along the sidewalk towards the office. Then his eyes caught the glint of something metallic on the approaching figure's chest.

"It's one of 'em!" Wade breathed, returning with featherlight steps to his position by the door.

Nearer came the sound of the feet and the door swung open. The waiting men saw the dark shape hesitate, while a muffled sound rose from it. Before they could think about his peculiar behaviour, the man came forward with a jerky motion as if shoved from the rear. Even if he had thought anything was wrong, Turner could not have prevented himself from moving. Tensed for the arrival, he swung his arm around and crashed the whip's handle on to the newcomer's head. Buckling at the knees, the victim went down on his face without making a sound.

"We got one of 'em!" Turner hissed triumphantly. "Light the lamp so we can see to tie him."

Having kicked the door shut as soon as the

man entered, Wade moved to follow his companion's suggestion. While their victim sprawled unmoving on the floor, he must be secured quickly. So Wade crossed to the desk, fumbled in his pants' pocket and took out a match. Tingling with excitement, he lit the lamp and started to turn towards the door.

Grinning confidently as the lamp flooded its light across the room, Turner looked down to discover which of the Texans lay at his feet. Strangely the full impact of what he saw did not strike him immediately. First he took in the fact that the wrists of the unconscious man were handcuffed behind him. Then he realized that a bandana, knotted around their victim's face was acting as a gag. Lastly he became aware of the re-cumbent figure's identity.

"Jackie!" he gasped.

Even as the word broke from Turner's lips, the door burst open violently.

Recalling that Doc had filled the lamps earlier in the evening, Dusty had read a warning significance from the darkened state of the office. He did not accept his prisoner's story of Doc being held in exchange for the deserters' release and wondered if he might also be a target for capture. If so, the office would be a good place to make such an attempt. Under normal conditions, it would be the last place to be suspected of harbouring enemies.

Quickly Dusty reached his decision. He brought Jackie to a halt and, before the youngster could protest, gagged him with his own bandana. Unpinning the badge from his shirt, Dusty fastened it on the other's vest. Then he gripped the back of Jackie's waistband and thrust the nose of his left hand Colt against the young man's spine.

"Start walking!" Dusty ordered, his voice low yet throbbing with controlled savagery. "Make any fuss for me, and it'll be the last thing you do."

Never the quickest of thinkers, Jackie failed to appreciate the danger or why his captor was acting in such a manner. One thing he did not doubt, that Dusty would carry out the threat. Wyatt Earp and most other Kansas lawmen were quite capable of shooting a defenceless man, so Jackie figured all peace officers to be equally callous. With that in mind, he continued walking towards the darkened office.

Then Jackie became aware of the way Dusty was escorting him. The small Texan gripped him by the waist band and moved directly behind him on silent feet. Vague, half-formed throughts crept into the youngster's head and he tried to stop. Instantly the Colt's muzzle gouged into his kidney area and he gave up the attempt.

Reaching the office door, Dusty holstered his Colt. If there should be men waiting inside, he must handle them without shooting. There was a chance that Doc was still alive, or that Jackie was telling the truth, in which case the sound of shooting from the office might alarm the men who held him and bring about his death. Dusty felt Jackie's body tense as he reached around it to open the door. Croaks of anxiety rose from the young man, muffled by the gag.

Before Jackie could make any determined objection and alert any waiting friends, Dusty shoved him forward. Down lashed an arm, holding a weapon of some kind, then the door jerked shut. That meant at least two of them, for the striker could not also have closed the door. Then Dusty heard voices and grinned savagely. Crouching on the sidewalk, he waited for the lamp to be lit. As light glowed inside the office, he hurled himself forward, kicked open the door and entered fast.

Startled by the sight of Jackie sprawled at

his feet, Turner staggered back a few steps as Dusty came in. Bounding over the recumbent figure, Dusty struck while still in the air. Around lashed his right arm, striking with the *uraken* back fist of *karate*. The projecting second knuckle impacted on Turner's nose with considerable force considering that Dusty was moving past the man as he hit him. Pain half-blinded Turner momentarily, sending him staggering backwards and causing him to drop the whip. It also kept him out of action and gave Dusty time to come to grips with Wade.

No less surprised than his companion at Dusty's dramatic appearance, Wade recovered slightly faster and sent his hand fanning towards its gun. However he failed to move quite fast enough. Landing beyond Jackie, after striking Turner, Dusty bounded across the office. While Wade's hand was still raising the Colt from its holster, Dusty closed and kicked him in the stomach. Breath burst from Wade's lungs as he doubled over, while his hand released the gun's butt. Swiftly Dusty linked his two hands, bringing them up under the outlaw's jaw which came forward to meet them. With a surging heave, he sent Wade back over the desk to crash on to the chair behind it. Collapsing under the man's weight, the chair deposited him on the floor.

Drawing a hand across his face, Turner glared at the blood smeared on to it from his throbbing nose. The sight caused him to forget his gun and he hurled forward determined to beat his assailant to a pulp. Reaching the small Texan just as Wade went over the desk, Turner decided against turning him around. Instead he encircled Dusty's neck with a powerful left arm from the rear, hooking the right hand to the left as an aid to strangling him.

Arching his back, Dusty carried his left foot forward and outwards to support his weight as he braced himself against Turner's pull to the rear. With his balance secured, Dusty twisted his hips to the right. He knew a clenched fist would not serve him at that moment, so prepared to use the *tegatana*, hand-sword. Hand open, with fingers extended together and thumb folded on the palm, he bent his right arm across his chest. Pivoting his torso to add force to the blow, he drove his arm down. The hard heel of his hand slashed between Turner's spread apart legs. Pain tore through the stocky hard-case as the ultra-sensitive area took what felt like the impact of a blunt meat-axe.

Dusty felt the arms loosen on his neck and tore free of them as he continued to turn. With Turner doubling over in agony, his jaw offered itself to the savage backhand swing launched by Dusty's left arm. Hard knuckles cracked solidly under the outlaw's jaw, snapping his head back and sending him sprawling across the room. Crashing to the floor, Turner just missed being struck by the door as it flew open.

Arriving at the Golden Nugget, Chesil failed to see any of his three absent colleagues. However he overheard a conversation which told him of Jackie's arrest by Dusty Fog. So he turned and left the saloon, joining the two men who were waiting reluctantly on the sidewalk.

"Fog's got Jackie," Chesil told Snell and Russon. "We'll have to get him out."

"He knows why we're here," Chesil pointed out.

"The hell with him!" Snell growled.

"He'll talk!" Russon stated. "Where's Wade 'n' Turner?"

"Not there," Chesil replied, starting to

walk along the street. "Let's go and free Jackie. We can grab off Fog at the same time."

"Could be they went after Fog instead of coming to meet you," Russon remarked as he and Snell followed on Chesil's heels.

A point which their leader had already thought of—and did not like.

Anger gripped Chesil as he stalked along the street towards the marshal's office. After much study, observation and planning, he had thought up a fool-proof scheme to rob the Farmers Bank. Everything had been going his way at first. Learning of the army deserters, he arranged that the law would also hear about them. While he had another plan, involving the return of the deserters to Fort Debdale, by which some of the deputies would be sent out of town, the Army had saved him the trouble. None of the gang guessed, and Chesil did not mean to tell them, but that part of the affair had been pure luck. So was the premature capture of Doc Leroy.

At which point the wheel had turned and pointed the arrow of fortune the other way. That stupid, useless kid, Jackie, had taken Doc Leroy's gunbelt where it could be seen and recognized by Dusty Fog. To a man as smart as the marshal of Trail End, there would be a grim significance in Leroy's capture. From the moment he learned of it, Dusty Fog would be on the alert. Should Wade and Turner have started thinking for themselves, deciding to lay their ambush at the marshal's office, they might ruin the whole scheme. With such knowledge at his disposal, Dusty Fog would not regard even his office as a safe area.

Cursing the luck which had brought him companions who "thought" for themselves instead of following orders, Chesil came into sight of the marshal's office. Instantly he knew his fears were justified. Lights glowed inside the building and he saw a figure hurl itself at the door.

"Come on!" he yelled. "Stick to the street!"

Doing so allowed them to run in comparative silence. Sufficient noise came from inside the office to cover the thud of their boots as they mounted and crossed the sidewalk. Eager to show his superiority, Snell charged by the others. Kicking the door open, he went through it with hand dropping towards his gun.

"No shooting!" Chesil yelled. "Take Fog alive!"

Any doubts Dusty felt about the identity of the new arrivals departed at the words. So he did not hesitate. Flinging himself forward, he rolled over the desk and dropped crouching behind it. Not far from him, Wade groaned and started to sit up. Concealed from the men at the door, Dusty knew he must act and fast. Pulling off his hat, he skimmed it up to strike and extinguish the lamp. At the same moment Wade lurched to his feet.

By the door, Snell saw the figure rising from beyond the desk. Believing it to be Dusty taking advantage of the sudden plunge into darkness, the outlaw forgot Chesil's instructions. Jerking out his gun, he fired and heard the soggy "whomp!" as its bullet struck human flesh.

Dusty saw the man behind him reel and fall. Drawing his right side Colt, he thrust himself from behind the desk. Flame sparked a glowing muzzle-blast towards the door. Letting out a cry of pain, Snell spun around, struck the side of the door and bounced from it into the other wall.

"Beat it!" Chesil snarled as Snell slipped downwards.

"Where to?" Russon asked, following his boss along the street.

"The hotel. I have to get my saddlebags before we pull out."

Cocking his Colt on its recoil, Dusty prepared to shoot again. Then he heard the sound of feet running away from the door. He rose cautiously, moving across the office, ready to start shooting at the first hostile sound. Apart from the muffled groans from Jackie, he saw no sign of any movement from the outlaws. Darting through the door, he ignored the people who were coming along the street to investigate the disturbance. All his attention fixed on the departing foot-falls.

"What's up?" yelled one of the men who ran towards the office.

Recognizing the voice as belonging to a man heartily in agreement with the clean up of the town, Dusty called back, "Trouble. Take care of the office."

Then the small Texan sprang off in pursuit of the departing outlaws, trying to keep the sound of their feet within hearing in the hope that they would lead him to a living, unharmed Doc Leroy.

"Now I ain't the complaining kind," said the fat man in the night-shirt, using a tone

Stoeger's night manager knew heralded the coming of a complaint. "But something's got to be done about the noise. Whoever's in the room over me's been stomping hell out of the floor and I can't sleep for it."

Certainly the protest had justification, the manager concluded, for a steady, almost mechanical thudding boomed from the floor of the room overhead. That would be the one occupied by the tinhorn who planned to run a poker game. While Mr. Chesil had paid well for the privilege, the complainant was a regular visitor and friend of the owner. That meant his complaint must take precedence over a bribe received from a transient gambler. Anyway, the bribe simply covered running a poker game and carried the proviso that no other guest must be inconvenienced by its players.

"I'll go up and see Mr. Chesil, sir," the manager promised.

Despite the importance of his position, the manager lacked the physical development to back up protests. Shortish, middle-aged, somewhat weedy in build, he had selected a weapon calculated to command respect. Thrust into his waistband, he carried a twin-barrel shot pistol. While only a twelve gauge, its double mouths formed a mighty effective inducement for complying with his requests. Stalking up the stairs with all the dignity of his post, the manager reached and knocked on the door of Chesil's room.

"Manager here!" he announced. "What's going on in there now?"

"Now that's a right smart question," Doc thought as the words reached his ears, and stamped with renewed vigour. "Come on, damn it, open up!"

"Now then, in there!" came the manager's voice. "If you don't quit that, I'll have to ask you to leave!"

"You won't get any arguments from me about that," Doc silently assured him, raising aching legs and propelling them down again.

"Dang it, manager!" yelled an indignant voice from below. "He's still at it!"

"That does it!" the manager warned in his most threatening tone. "I'm coming in there right now!"

"And about time, too!" Doc breathed.

Drawing and cocking his shot pistol ready to quell any objections from the room's occupants, the manager used his pass-key to unlock the door. With the gun held so that its full potential could be seen and appreciated, the man entered the room. He slammed to a halt, staring at the bound figure on the bed. Despite the gag and blindfold hiding most of the features, he recognized the prisoner.

"Deputy Leroy!" he yelped, heading for the bed. "What're you doing here?"

"What the hell do you think I'm doing," Doc fumed, bouncing up and down on the bed to emphasize his gagged comment, "waiting for a stagecoach?"

In his haste to free Doc, the manager set the pistol, without lowering its hammers, down on the bed. Then he pulled up the blindfold and unfastened the gag.

"What happ—" the manager began.

"Cut me free, *pronto*!" Doc growled, screwing up his eyes in an effort to clear them and shield them from the sudden light. "There's going to be a bank robbery."

"Who did this to you?" the manager asked, opening a knife he took from his pants' pocket.

"I dunno, but I hope I get my hands on them!"

Swiftly the knife sliced through the ropes about Doc's arms. Cursing a little at the stiffness, Doc knew he had been fortunate. Wearing his jacket had prevented the blood's circulation from being cut off and use returned rapidly to his limbs. Knuckling his eyes dry, he glanced at the manager kneeling to free his feet. Doc saw the shot pistol, noticed its cocked condition and opened his mouth to mention the matter. Then he heard running feet in the passage and the door, which had swung almost closed of its own accord, jerked open.

Chesil saw the door to his room standing ajar as he and Russon reached the head of the stairs. Realizing that something had gone wrong, the gang leader let his companion take the lead. Flight might have been the safest plan, but the saddle bags held money and other items Chesil would rather not fall into the hands of the law while he still lived. So he let Russon go in front, the better to estimate the extent of the danger.

At the sight of Doc sitting partially free on the bed, Russon skidded to a halt and grabbed for his Colt. Doc's left hand came up into the manager's face and shoved, sending him toppling over backwards. At the same moment, the slender right hand closed around the shot pistol's butt. There was no time to take careful aim, nor need with such a weapon. Giving an awesome bellow, the left hand barrel belched out its load. A spreading cloud of bird-shot laced its path across the room, driving into Russon's chest with a force that hurled him bodily through the door.

Fighting down the wicked recoil kick of the pistol, Doc knew he need not fire again. No man could stand up with a hole larger than a human fist driven through his breast bone.

Seeing Russon pitch backwards out of the room, Chesil forgot any idea of collecting the saddlebags. They contained enough to hang him, but the need would not arise if he tried to go through the door. That had been a shotgun of some kind. No other weapon possessed such a devastating effect. No man could match a revolver against a shot gun and hope to stay alive.

With that in mind, Chesil turned and ran towards the stairs. If he could reach the streets, escape was still possible. The horses were waiting for him and he could build up a good start over any pursuit. Given the hours of darkness, during which tracking was impossible, he hoped to be twenty miles from Trail End by dawn.

Half-way down the stairs, he saw a man come into the hotel lobby. A small, insignificant man with dusty blond hair and the dress of a Texas cowhand. Or so he might appear at first glance. Not any more to Chesil, for he knew Dusty Fog.

Down flashed the outlaw's hand, in a move which had brought him through more than one disagreement. To Chesil's mind, there were few who could equal his speed and he almost relished the chance to match himself against another of the fast-draw clan.

Although an instant after Chesil in starting his draw, Dusty's left side Colt came into his right hand while the other's was still being lifted clear of the holster. From waist high, the Colt bucked against Dusty's palm and its bullet drove between Chesil's eyes. Rocking backwards, Chesil fell on to the stairs. His revolver roared as he went down, ploughing a hole in the floor at Dusty's feet. Then the outlaw's fingers opened and his weapon slipped from them. Slowly his body slid to the foot of the stairs.

Leaping forward, filled with anxiety for Doc's safety, Dusty bounded up the stairs. He ran along the passage, oblivious of the heads which emerged cautiously from various doorways, and hardly glancing at Russon's body as he entered Chesil's room.

Seeing his friend, Doc started to rise. Then the slim Texan let out a low groaning curse and sank on to the bed again.

"Are you all right, Doc?" Dusty asked worriedly.

"No," Doc replied with feeling. "My feet ache like hell."

Tired, dust-smeared and showing signs of hard riding, Mark Counter, the Ysabel Kid and Waco entered the marshal's office at half past seven on Tuesday morning. Indignation showed on their faces as they came to a halt and stared at the scene which greeted them. Feet on its top, arms folded and hat drawn over his eyes, Dusty sat sleeping at the desk. At the left of the door, Doc reclined on a bench and also slept.

"Well don't that beat all?" demanded the Kid. "We ride ourselves thin getting back here in case we're needed, and we find this pair sleeping like bears in winter."

Slowly Dusty shoved back his hat and eyed the trio coldly. What with Doc attending to the wounded Wade, patching up Jackie's lacerated skull and guarding the prisoners, Dusty had spent almost the whole night on the rounds. In fact they had only just settled down to grab some sleep about half an hour back.

"Make less noise and leave us get some rest," he told the trio. "These quiet Mondays are sure hell."

THE END

GUIDE
TO THE COLOUR CODING
OF
ULVERSCROFT BOOKS

Many of our readers have written to us expressing their appreciation for the way in which our colour coding has assisted them in selecting the Ulverscroft books of their choice. To remind everyone of our colour coding— this is as follows:

BLACK COVERS
Mysteries

*

BLUE COVERS
Romances

*

RED COVERS
Adventure Suspense and General Fiction

*

ORANGE COVERS
Westerns

*

GREEN COVERS
Non-Fiction

WESTERN TITLES
in the
Ulverscroft Large Print Series

Gone To Texas	*Forrest Carter*
Dakota Boomtown	*Frank Castle*
Hard Texas Trail	*Matt Chisholm*
Bigger Than Texas	*William R. Cox*
From Hide and Horn	*J. T. Edson*
Gunsmoke Thunder	*J. T. Edson*
The Peacemakers	*J. T. Edson*
Wagons to Backsight	*J. T. Edson*
Arizona Ames	*Zane Grey*
The Lost Wagon Train	*Zane Grey*
Nevada	*Zane Grey*
Rim of the Desert	*Ernest Haycox*
Borden Chantry	*Louis L'Amour*
Conagher	*Louis L'Amour*
The First Fast Draw *and*	
The Key-Lock Man	*Louis L'Amour*
Kiowa Trail *and* Killoe	*Louis L'Amour*
The Mountain Valley War	*Louis L'Amour*
The Sackett Brand *and*	
The Lonely Men	*Louis L'Amour*
Taggart	*Louis L'Amour*
Tucker	*Louis L'Amour*
Destination Danger	*Wm. Colt MacDonald*

MYSTERY TITLES
in the
Ulverscroft Large Print Series